M000203394

SUGAR AND VICE

CUPCAKE TRUCK MYSTERIES BOOK 1

EMILY JAMES

STRONGHOLD BOOKS

Copyright © 2018 by Emily James

All rights reserved.

No part of this publication may be reproduced, distributed, or transmitted in any form or by any means, including photocopying, recording, or other electronic or mechanical methods, without the prior written permission of the author. It's okay to quote a small section for a review or in a school paper. To put this in plain language, this means you can't copy my work and profit from it as if it were your own. When you copy someone's work, it's stealing. No one likes a thief, so don't do it. Pirates are not nearly as cool in real life as they are in fiction.

For permission requests, write to the author at the address below.

Emily James

authoremilyjames@gmail.com

www.authoremilyjames.com

This is a work of fiction. I made it up. You are not in my book. I probably don't even know you. If you're confused about the difference between real life and fiction, you might want to call a counselor rather than a lawyer because names, characters, places, and incidents in this book are a product of my twisted imagination. Real locales and public names are sometimes used for atmospheric purposes. Any resemblance to actual people, living or dead, or to businesses, companies, events, and institutions is completely coincidental.

Editor: Christopher Saylor at www.saylorediting.wordpress.com/services/

Cover Design: Mariah Sinclair at www.mariahsinclair.com

Published September 2018 by Stronghold Books

Print Book ISBN: 978-1-988480-24-4

ALSO BY EMILY JAMES

Maple Syrup Mysteries

Cupcake Truck Mysteries

Dead Velvet Cake (coming soon!)

FREE TIPS FOR AMAZING CUPCAKES

 Each book in the Cupcake Truck Mysteries includes a cupcake recipe, but even when you have a great recipe, baking the perfect cupcake can sometimes be hard.

To receive the top 10 tips for amazing cupcakes (inspired by the Cupcake Truck Mysteries sleuth, Isabel), sign up for my newsletter at www.subscribepage.com/cupcakes.

(If you're already a member of my newsletter, no need to worry. I've emailed you a link to the tips too!)

CHAPTER 1

After a year of running my cupcake truck, I was beginning to think my motto should be *Never trust a client.*

Or, at least, never trust a client when they tell me what they'll have on site for me to create my cupcake display.

When Claire Cartwright hired me to provide cupcakes for her grandfather's massive 100th birthday party, she'd assured me they'd have "everything I needed" to set up my display. Everything I needed apparently only included two bare picnic tables.

My second mistake after trusting that what I'd need would be on site was asking Claire about it.

She planted her hands on hips narrow enough to tell me she probably rarely ate a cupcake. "Of course we wouldn't have anything else here," she said. "That's your job, not mine."

It often *was* my job, which was why I'd confirmed with her

twice that I'd only be required to bring the cupcakes, lay them out, and stay to serve them if asked. Decorating hadn't been part of our verbal contract.

But I'd already overheard Claire threatening not to pay the food truck vendor catering the hot dogs and hamburgers if they ran out of fried onions for the burgers. I couldn't afford to have her not pay me because I failed to provide a display. After the lean winter months, my cupcake truck was one flat tire or mechanical malfunction away from going under. I probably should have weathered the winter in the town of Fair Haven, where I already had established clients. But it hadn't felt safe anymore.

Hindsight is only useful for making you regret the choices you'd made, though. Right now, I needed a practical solution. "There's enough space here for me to pull my truck up and serve the guests that way. Would that be alright?"

"Obviously not." Claire's lip practically curled. "This isn't a baseball game."

Before she could get any more riled up, I stepped back and dipped my head in a sign of submission. In my experience, most battles weren't worth fighting. "I'll figure something out, and it'll be ready as promised before your guests finish their first hotdog."

"It better be. I refuse to pay for services that aren't properly rendered."

She tossed me a look that suggested she didn't have time to

deal with my incompetence anymore and scurried off toward where a young man on a ladder hung streamers from the gazebo.

If I screwed this up, I'd never see a nickel of what I was owed. The reasonable woman who'd hired me for this job seemed to have transformed into the birthday party form of a bridezilla.

Unfortunately, I didn't keep display material stored in my truck. I might have been able to if I wasn't also living in it, but my sleeping bag, portable heater, and few other personal items ate up any extra room.

I had passed a dollar store not too far away. It seemed like my best bet to get the supplies I'd need to salvage this.

If nothing else, it had to be better than putting cupcakes out onto naked picnic tables. I was pretty sure I'd noticed some white spots that could only be bird poop on the wood.

Now the question was whether I could pull it all together and set up my cupcakes in the time remaining to me before the party was scheduled to begin.

———

THE MOMENT I PULLED BACK INTO THE PARKING LOT, I KNEW MY promise to Claire to have the cupcake display ready before the guests were looking for dessert would be impossible to fulfill. Harold Cartwright's progeny seemed to have a genetic predisposition to punctuality.

Cars filled the parking lot even though the party wasn't scheduled to begin for almost an hour. I had to park my truck at the edge farthest from the park because all the closer spaces where I could fit were filled.

Arms piled with my dollar-store haul, I speed-walked back to my designated tables.

By the time I set down my load onto my two picnic tables, the other food vendor wore a look that said he regretted ever taking this job. Claire was hassling him about the fact that four containers of ketchup and six squeeze bottles of mustard wouldn't be enough to serve the two hundred or more people she expected.

I almost snipped off a finger with the scissors I was using to cut the plastic stems off the dollar-store flowers. Two hundred people. Fifty more than what she'd commissioned me to provide cupcakes for. I always rounded orders up since some people would take more than one, and often more people showed up for events than expected. But fifty additional *planned for* people that I didn't know about left me with no wiggle room.

I was starting to think Claire Cartwright hired me despite my being a relative newcomer to town because none of the established businesses would work with her.

Whatever her reasons, I needed the money. Starvation and the threat of losing my truck motivated me to tolerate a lot.

I organized my supplies, my stomach turning itself into a boiling pot of nerves as guests congregated around where they would queue up for their hotdogs and burgers. The photographer Claire had hired to document the event was already snapping pictures. Time was not on my side.

I needed to glue the candlesticks to the platters to create a multi-tiered display. The only problem was, Super Sticky glue had to have pressure applied to it while it set. Otherwise, I risked my display crumbling under the weight of my cupcakes if anyone so much as brushed it with their sleeve. I couldn't stand around and hold each piece together as the glue hardened. I needed to transport my trays of cupcakes from my truck.

I also wasn't about to ask anyone for help. Claire seemed like the kind of woman who wouldn't appreciate me putting her guests to work. Besides that, I preferred it when people noticed my cupcakes and forgot about me. One of the best ways to make sure Jarrod never found me was to remain invisible or easily forgettable.

The next best thing to a human holding the pieces together would be to use something heavy. Since the hotdogs and hamburgers had only just gone on the grills, I sneaked over and grabbed up the five ketchup containers and a few of the mustard bottles. The hotdog vendor was clearly as scared of not being paid by Claire as I was because he'd somehow managed to produce additional condiments since Claire's lecture.

I couldn't help but wonder if he'd now get another lecture because the new bottles of ketchup were a different brand from the ones originally set out. It sounded like the kind of thing that might set Claire off, especially since the newest bottles were a cheap generic brand and the originals were some fancy specialty ketchup.

Once I had everything glued and weighted down, I sprinted back across the parking lot. Thank goodness Michigan was cooler in early May than Florida was. Had I been jogging around outside in Florida right now, I'd be a sweaty mess not fit to serve food to anyone.

By the time I got back with my first tray to the spot in the park where Harold Cartwright's party was taking place, even more guests had arrived. The line for food snaked out of sight behind the gazebo, and a group of around ten children ages six to twelve played a game of Red Rover while waiting for their families to reach the front of the line.

Someone had removed the ketchup and mustard bottles from my display, and they now sat back in their place next to the relish. With everyone already lined up to eat, I didn't have long before they'd be coming my way for dessert.

I shifted position to keep my back to the photographer as he moved closer to my area and wiggled my display. Whoever had removed the ketchup bottles had left them there long enough for the glue to set at least. I quickly glued the flowers and stones in a way that hid the spots where the candlesticks connected to the serving trays. I didn't bother holding them in place while the glue set.

I arranged my cupcakes, sprinted back to my truck, and returned with another tray.

I'd already set out the raspberry cupcakes with white chocolate frosting, my coconut with mango curd tropical cupcakes, and the s'mores cupcakes—all popular warm-weather selections. All that I still had to carry were the specially requested carrot cake cupcakes made without nuts because the guest of honor was allergic and carrot cake was his favorite.

Given that the guests were already eating, I piled my arms full with the remaining three trays from my truck. My eyes barely peeked over the top, and I knew my arms would ache tomorrow. The stack had to weigh 20 or 30 pounds.

I carefully picked my way through the parking lot. I came around the back of the final van before the cement gave way to grass. A man appeared seemingly out of nowhere and crashed into me.

Hard.

My three trays of carrot cake cupcakes flew into the air.

CHAPTER 2

I stumbled sideways from the impact, sure I was going to end up on the ground beside my cupcakes. The man grabbed my upper arm, keeping me on my feet.

"Are you all right?" he asked.

I wasn't. I wouldn't be as long as his hand was on my arm. Because, for a second, I wasn't standing in front of a man ten years my junior who'd run into me in a parking lot. It was Jarrod's face I saw, and Jarrod's hand on my arm keeping me from escaping.

"Ma'am?"

Stay calm, Amy...err, Isabel. I had to remember to think about myself as Isabel. If I didn't, one day I'd slip up in my speech as well.

Stay calm, Isabel. This man isn't Jarrod.

Adrenaline continued to race through my body, making me

feel as if I'd drunk three pots of coffee today rather than a single cup.

I edged away far enough to force him to release my arm. "I'm fine."

He glanced back toward the park in a way the sent another rush of nervous energy crashing over me. It was the motion of someone who didn't want to be seen.

"Do you need help bringing this"—he waved a hand at the disaster that used to be my trays of cupcakes—"back to your car?"

Why wouldn't he have simply asked if I needed help? He might not be Jarrod, but for all I knew, Jarrod had hired him to bump into me as a ruse to lure me away from other people.

"No thanks. I've got this."

He backed up a step. "You sure?" Another step backward. "I'm really sorry."

I nodded, and he spun on his heel and trotted away. My heart slowed down to a semi-normal rhythm. It was much more likely that he'd stopped by to say happy birthday to Harold Cartwright and wanted to make his exit before anyone spotted him and wanted a long chat. It wasn't unusual for people to pop into one of these events for a few minutes, just to say they'd come, and then leave.

That's what I had to tell myself, anyway, or I wouldn't have enough presence of mind left to deal with the fact that three trays of cupcakes lay on the ground around me. And not any three trays. The three trays of specially requested carrot cake cupcakes.

One of the trays had burst open completely. The cupcakes lay scattered on the ground around me like pieces of oversized confetti. One had even landed in a puddle of black goo that looked suspiciously like engine oil.

I couldn't entirely abandon these three trays, though. I wouldn't have enough cupcakes, and I'd also not have the one flavor Claire said was essential. Two of my trays had landed lid-side down, but at least the lids had stayed on and the cupcakes were still inside.

I flipped them over and popped the top. I couldn't hold back a groan. The contents of my trays were a mangled mass, most of the icing stuck to the underside of the lid. I didn't have enough ingredients to re-make the cream cheese icing and re-ice them. Trying to salvage them in their current form wasn't an option.

Claire Cartwright was going to stiff me on my payment for sure.

I covered the two trays, gathered up the third now-empty one, and scurried for my truck.

Somehow, I had to create more carrot cake cupcakes out of thin air.

HALF AN HOUR LATER, I POWER-WALKED BACK TO THE PARTY,

paying careful attention to my surroundings so no rogue men ran into me a second time. If I lost the solution I'd come up with, I'd be out of luck.

With the cupcakes and icing already smashed together, I'd peeled the liners off and turned them into cake pops.

They weren't carrot cake cupcakes, but hopefully I could pass them off to Claire Cartwright as being even better. And hopefully Harold Cartwright didn't hate white chocolate.

The guests were clustered to the side of where they'd been lined up for food, most of their backs facing my direction as I approached.

A tingle traced down my neck. Unless all the guests moved and ate with military precision and had now gathered to sing "Happy Birthday" to Harold Cartwright, they shouldn't have already been finished going through the food line. I knew they weren't there to watch him cut a cake. I was the one and only dessert.

Fear told me to turn around, go back to my truck, and leave. Fear and I were what the generation after me called frenemies. He often helped keep me safe. He used to warn me about when to try to stay out of Jarrod's way. He'd helped keep me quiet when I wanted to talk back. I'd probably be dead now if not for him.

But he'd also made me run from a place I'd started to feel comfortable, even though it might have been better for me to stay. He kept me from having any friendships, always telling me friends would get me or them or both of us killed. He'd cost me more hours of sleep than were healthy for anyone to miss.

And, in this case, he threatened to cost me a job I desperately needed the money from. If Claire Cartwright decided not to pay me, I'd have to cut back to one meal a day.

So this time—at least for the moment—I stuck my metaphorical fingers in my ears and refused to listen to him.

I continued on to my cupcake display. Hungry partygoers had already decimated what I'd set out earlier.

"Do something, Dan," a voice that sounded like Claire's said from the direction of the crowd. "Help him."

Said might've been a generous way of describing her words. Her voice was more of a screech. A very panicked screech.

My hands trembled, and I set my cake pops down on the picnic table before I could drop them.

Up close, I could see that the crowd wasn't just gathered. Some of the adults hugged children close, while others were talking on their cell phones. None of them were smiling.

I inched toward the fringe of the crowd, but there were too many people between me and what was happening for me to see anything. I dropped into a squat instead. It'd be easier to see between legs. I certainly wasn't going to push any closer, drawing attention to myself and potentially getting trapped in the crowd. All I needed to know was what was happening so I could decide whether to stay or go.

A man about my age—mid to late 30s—knelt on the grass

next to a prone figure. The cane lying beside them, along with the Velcro-close orthopedic shoes, told me the person on the ground was the guest of honor, Harold Cartwright.

Poor Claire. Poor everyone who'd come to celebrate what was supposed to be a happy milestone. As much as Claire had been a touch unreasonable, I wouldn't have wished this on her or on the other party-goers.

I climbed to my feet and eased backward.

What were the odds that Harold Cartwright would die at his own birthday party? Theoretically, it was possible. He was a hundred, after all. And maybe I was simply paranoid because I spent most of my time expecting Jarrod to find me. The excitement alone could have caused Harold's old heart to stop.

But it seemed a bit too coincidental.

Definitely time for me to leave. No one was likely to be interested in food anymore. Anyone who was could get a cupcake for themselves. I'd fulfilled my obligation. I'd provided everything asked, some things I hadn't been asked for, and I even managed to get carrot cake onto the table. Sort of. I'd quickly put the cake pops out before I left. That way Claire couldn't short me because I hadn't provided the full count.

Police and ambulance were likely on their way already, and if anything looked fishy about the way Harold died, there'd be questions. I wasn't about to appear in a police report for the sake of a man I'd only met today, even if it was only as a witness. Jarrod could access police reports. If he ever figured out my new name, I didn't want to show up in any database, telling him where to find me.

I turned toward my picnic tables.

A little girl who couldn't have been more than four or five hunched on the ground next to one of the picnic table benches. Her chest rose and fell with the gaspy motions of someone struggling to breathe, and her cheeks were flushed an unnatural pink. One strap of a backpack hung partly off her shoulder.

This had to be so scary for a child. She might not even understand what was happening. She'd only know it wasn't good.

My heart tightened in the way that reminded me of someone trying to squeeze juice from an uncooperative orange. When I was a little girl myself and I'd asked my dad why my chest felt that way sometimes, he'd told me it was God squeezing compassion out of my heart for others. I knew now that wasn't the truth, but the memory made me both want to smile and to cry. I might be a lot better off now if I could still tap into my dad's wisdom.

At least I knew what he'd say about the little girl. I'd get her a cupcake and reassure her before I left. It put me at risk of the police showing up, but I couldn't leave her there, scared and alone, while the adults were focused on Harold. No one, no matter their age, should have to be scared and alone.

I hurried over to her, grabbed two different cupcakes, and

dropped to one knee beside her. "You know what makes me feel better? A treat."

My dad couldn't look down on me from heaven, but if he could, he'd be shaking his head and telling me I shouldn't be teaching a child to cope with stress using food. But I didn't know what else to do to calm her down. My experience with children was limited. My baby hadn't taken a full breath.

She raised her little face to me. Sweat plastered her fine blonde hair to her forehead.

The cupcakes slipped from my hands. Growing up in a home with a religious dad, I'd been raised not to curse, but I really wanted to right now.

She wasn't flushed and breathing hard because she was scared. A rash covered her cheeks, and her breathing had the type of rasp to it that I'd heard when my dad was stung by a wasp. It was the one that said her airways were closing down and soon she wouldn't be able to breathe at all.

CHAPTER 3

This family was cursed. Or the zombie apocalypse was starting with them. The farther and faster I could get away from them, the better.

Except now I couldn't leave. If she were having an allergic reaction, it would have had to happen after Harold Cartwright's collapse took all the adult attention. Someone would have noticed otherwise. That meant her reaction was a severe one, progressing fast. Even with emergency personnel on the way, they might not get here in time.

If she was having an anaphylactic reaction the way my dad had, we might not even have time to find her parents. Anaphylaxis needed immediate treatment with an epi pen.

I wiped her damp hair back from her forehead. Her skin was warm to the touch. "Do you know if you have allergies to anything, sweetie?"

"Nuts." The word wheezed out. "Daddy says I always have to ask if things have nuts or touched nuts, even if I don't see any."

Nuts were a common enough allergy, but there shouldn't have been anything with nuts in it at Harold Cartwright's party. He was allergic as well, hence why I'd had to leave the nuts out of the carrot cake cupcakes.

I glanced back over my shoulder to where Harold lay. Maybe someone really had wanted to take out a hundred-year-old man. Either that or the other food vendor had a weird recipe for making hamburgers and hot dogs that included peanut butter.

That sounded crazy even to me, and gross, but the little girl did have ketchup residue at the corners of her mouth. She'd eaten either a hamburger or a hotdog not that long ago.

"Do you have special medicine that you're supposed to take? It probably looks like a little tube—the size of a marker."

I moved my fingers apart to show her how big it would be.

She nodded, but she couldn't seem to get anything more out.

If she were my little girl, I wouldn't have kept the epi pen in my purse or anywhere that she might be without it. I'd make her carry it with her.

I stripped off the pink backpack she wore. My hands shook so hard I almost couldn't get ahold of the zipper above the unicorn's head.

I rummaged through the main pouch, but it didn't hold an epi pen.

Of course not. It'd be too easy to fall out there.

I wrenched open a smaller side pouch. An epi pen lay inside.

The girl slouched against me now. I couldn't tell if she were breathing or not.

Blue to the sky, orange to the thigh was the mantra my dad and I learned when he first found out he was allergic to wasps and needed to carry an epi pen.

It was a myth that an epi pen couldn't be used through clothes, but I did need to be able to insert the needle at a ninety-degree angle into her thigh and hold it there for ten seconds. I laid her on the ground.

"This might pinch, but you have to stay super still for me."

Hopefully she wasn't panicking so much that she couldn't obey. I popped the safety cap and pinned her leg down with my hip just in case.

"Hey!" a woman's voice yelled. "What are you doing?"

I stuck the girl with the pen and pressed until I felt the click. Then counted in my head.

"Get away from her!"

The woman was rushing toward me now, followed by a few others. My whole body screamed for me to run, but I couldn't let go. And I couldn't answer them. I didn't want to risk losing count in my head.

The woman's glance dropped to the pen, and her expression shifted, her eyes growing large. She pressed her hands to her mouth.

I hit the ten count and released my hold on the girl.

Hopefully, I'd been quick enough. With severe allergic reactions, the sooner you administered the epi pen, the more likely you were to stop the reaction.

"That's Janie, isn't it?" another woman said. "Dan's Janie."

Dan was the name of the man Claire called for to help Harold Cartwright, presumably because he had some medical training. No wonder no one noticed Janie's allergic reaction. Her dad was otherwise occupied, and for whatever reason, her mom wasn't around. Or her mom might be helping her dad.

None of which really mattered. An adrenaline crash often left my thoughts scattered to the wind, and I could feel it happening to me now. I'd been on an adrenaline rollercoaster most of today, and it was fading from my body again, leaving me feeling like there wasn't anything left inside but air. What I wanted to do was crawl into a corner and sleep it off. What I needed to do was make sure Janie would be alright and then get out of here.

And the practicalities of life had always had to take precedence over what I wanted.

I shifted and leaned closer to Janie's face. Her eyes were closed and wet tracks down her cheeks told me she'd been crying, but her breathing had eased somewhat. "You'll start to feel better now, and I'll make sure someone lets your daddy know. Okay?"

She nodded.

At least she was still conscious. That was a good sign.

I held out the hand clutching the epi pen and someone took it from me. "You need to call another ambulance for her. She may need a second dose, and sometimes there can be a weird, delayed reaction again a couple of hours later."

At least that's what they'd told us for my dad. The more severe the initial reaction, the more likely it was that someone would have a secondary reaction a few hours later, even without additional exposure to the allergen. Because he'd had other pre-existing conditions, they'd actually kept my dad in the hospital overnight.

It'd turned out they'd been right, and it'd also turned out that it didn't matter. The second attack put too much stress on his already-weak heart.

The woman who'd originally hollered at me knelt down next to Janie on her other side, and I climbed to my feet. My body felt like it was running on a pre-programmed sequence as I unloaded the cake pops from my tray. It was probably silly bothering to put them out, but I had to fulfill my obligation.

"Was that the cupcake lady?" a man asked as I walked away. "I think Janie'd have died if she hadn't acted fast the way she did."

There was no way the people who'd rushed over would forget what had happened. By saving Janie, I'd gone from a server—who most people wouldn't recognize if they passed them on the street the next day—to a quasi-hero.

I wasn't a hero. I'd simply done what needed to be done. And it was going to cost me. They'd tell the story of what had happened.

It might or might not get me more business. It would definitely get me too much attention.

As soon as Claire Cartwright paid me, I needed to consider leaving town.

Two days later, as I was setting up my food truck on a side street near the downtown, I dropped the *consider* and changed my stance to *I need to leave town.*

I'd figured out that this street was the perfect spot to catch lunch traffic. Food trucks weren't allowed to park for longer than 30 minutes in the limited downtown street parking in Lakeshore, and competition for those spaces was fierce. When I'd walked the area to check it out, I'd seen two vendors come to blows because one felt the other had taken his regular spot.

It didn't matter how much money could be made from those spots. I wasn't about to get into a fight, verbal or otherwise, for them. Plus, most people didn't want to buy a cupcake as their only lunch. I didn't think I could make 30 minutes financially viable.

But, other than the food trucks, the downtown was mostly businesses and shops. The restaurants frequented by the people working there tended to be a couple streets over. It took me a few days of watching the traffic patterns, but I'd spotted a location on a side street that the majority of the foot traffic passed by on their way to lunch. Since cupcakes were more of a dessert thing, that also meant they passed by me on their way back, and I'd already developed a contingent of regulars who picked up a cupcake for the afternoon slump.

My cell phone rang as I was pushing open the front flap, signifying I was open for business.

I locked the flap into place and swiped my finger across the screen to answer. "How Sweet It Is Cupcake Truck. Isabel speaking."

"Are you the cupcake truck that catered the hundredth birthday party for Harold Cartwright?" a man's voice asked.

I doubted Claire had recommended me to anyone. This morning's paper had an article about the tragic death of Harold Cartwright at his own hundredth birthday party. Claire would still be grieving. If she were in charge of Harold's estate, she'd also be making funeral plans, arranging for the reading of the will, sorting through his belongings, and trying to organize all the government paperwork.

Even if she had the chance to recommend me, being the cupcake truck who catered the party where Harold Cartwright died was hardly a glowing recommendation that would make people want to hire me, unless they were hiring me to cater the luncheon for a funeral.

It seemed more likely that whoever was calling was another

reporter, wanting some eyewitness quotes to go along with his follow-up story. The original article hadn't explicitly said so, but the wording implied that there would be an investigation to determine whether Harold had died of natural causes or not. Reporters tended to milk any hint of foul play and scandal for all it was worth.

I couldn't risk offending an actual potential client, though. "I'm sorry. I didn't catch your name."

"Alan Brooksbank. I'm a reporter for the *Lakeshore Daily*. I do have the right food truck, don't I?"

He'd admitted to being a reporter awfully easily. I'd half expected him to give me his name but pretend he was a potential client or to give me an entirely fake name in case I would recognize his from the paper. Maybe my response had tipped him to the fact that I wasn't going to be fooled by either of those ploys.

Since he'd been forthright with me, I'd be forthright with him. "I was one of the trucks catering the event, yes, but I didn't see anything. Even if I had, I think families should be left alone with their grief without the media causing rampant speculation about what might have happened."

Silence filled the other end of the line, and I cringed. That'd come out a lot harsher than I'd intended.

"I understand and respect that." He cleared his throat. "Those aren't the type of articles I write. I'm the Positivity Project columnist. All my articles are good news."

Great. Now I felt like a real jerk. This guy was doing exactly what my dad always said reporters should do more of. Yeah, we needed to know the truth about what was happening in the world, and that meant the bad stuff, too. But my dad always felt there should be an equal balance of good in the news because there was good happening all the time in the world.

There was a time when I agreed with him. Older, grown-up me had gotten a bit jaded, though, thinking that people only wanted to read about the blood and violence the same way gawkers snarled up traffic when there was an accident. Then I'd found the Positivity Project. It helped me keep hoping that tomorrow would be a better day and reminded me that not everyone was like Jarrod.

"I'm a fan of your column," I said lamely. "Sorry I didn't recognize your name right away. I'm just not sure why you're calling me. A cupcake makes every day better, but that's not enough to write a column about."

He chuckled. The paper didn't have a picture of him to go along with his column, but that laugh and his career choice made me think he must have dimples, a full head of untamable hair, and a permanent smile. Lean, athletic, and probably still in his early twenties, right out of school.

"I can always tell the ones who are going to make my job hard by being too modest," he said, the laugh still in his voice. "My sources told me that you made sure another life wasn't lost at Harold Cartwright's birthday party. You saved—" There was a bit of rustle and clatter in the background like he was moving things around on a metal desk, looking for a handwritten note. "You saved Harold's great-granddaughter Janie Holmes from dying from an allergy attack."

I knew it was bad when so many people spotted me. I never would have imagined it would get even worse by a reporter contacting me. "I recognized it as an allergy attack, and I knew what to do. That's not exactly story-worthy."

"Saving a little girl's life is pretty special. Besides, it'd be great publicity for your truck."

If I were anyone else, in any other situation, I'd have been flattered. In fact, I'd have jumped at the free marketing for my truck. The more people who knew about a business, and heard positive things about it, the higher income tended to be.

Instead, his insistence made me feel queasy. The last thing I wanted was my name and picture in the paper. I'd been reading the column long enough to know that he wouldn't be satisfied with a picture of my truck. The photos that went along with his articles featured smiling faces. He'd want a picture of me with Janie.

I couldn't have a picture of me in any paper, especially since the *Lakeshore Daily* had an online version. I was certain Jarrod would have a program set up to recognize my face if I showed up anywhere online.

None of that was something I could tell Alan Brooksbank. As *The Incredibles* had wisely said, your most valuable possession was your identity. I had to guard it at all costs.

What could I tell him to get him to back off? "Normally I'd be thrilled, but right now it would make me feel like I was benefiting from the family in their time of grief."

"I think the family would like to have the focus be on something happy that came from that day as well."

Had to give him points for persistence. "I'm not willing to take that risk."

"What if I checked with the family first?"

This man had no quit in him. Part of me admired it. The other part knew he'd be trouble if I gave him any encouragement. "I have customers I need to take care of, but thanks for thinking of me. I really do love your column."

I disconnected the call. Sometimes you had to be a little rude when your survival was on the line.

Sometimes you have to lie, too, Fear whispered in my head.

Knowing he was right didn't make me feel better about how often I lied to people in big and little ways. Even my name was a lie.

I hung out my chalkboard sign of the day's available cupcakes before any customers actually showed up. Each day, I alternated between having chocolate and vanilla cupcakes on the menu, since those were the two perennial favorites, and then I'd bake up two less-traditional flavors to keep people coming back to try something new. I drew a little picture beside each flavor to give people a hint of what they were in case the name didn't make it obvious.

Today I drew a white flower beside the vanilla, a cup of steaming coffee, and a lemon.

Two of my regulars walked by and waved.

"Save me a tiramisu, Isabel!" one of them called out, a grin on her face.

Then they went right back into their chatter. The all-too-familiar bite of loneliness gnawed at the edges of my heart.

I kicked it down and made sure I attached the name *Reporter* to Alan Brooksbank's phone number in my cell. If he called again, I'd let it go to voicemail.

And before my customers showed up, I'd call Claire Cartwright to ask her when I could pick up my payment. I'd planned to give her at least a week before contacting her, out of respect for her loss, but with a reporter poking around, time was a luxury I no longer had. As the old phrase said, it was time to get the heck out of Dodge. Or, in this case, the heck out of Lakeshore.

CHAPTER 4

A week later, I opened up the Positivity Project column on my phone, and a picture of my truck filled my screen. My hand went numb, and I lost my grip on my phone. It tumbled into my lap, barely missing sliding off onto the metal floor of my truck.

Alan Brooksbank wrote the article anyway, without my permission and without a quote from me. I'd ignored three of his calls this week. He'd left a voicemail the first two times. His initial call was him trying to convince me to meet with him for an interview. I'd deleted the second voicemail without listening to it, assuming it was more of the same. He hadn't left one on the third.

I should have listened to his second message. He probably said he was going forward with the article. He seemed like a nice guy for a reporter, so he might have even asked that I call him if I had any other objections. If I'd listened to that message and called him back, I might have convinced him to write about something or someone else instead.

Though that seemed unlikely, given how determined he'd been to write about what happened, and I couldn't go back in time—even if I could have, there were a lot of other things I'd have wanted to change first.

I sucked in a couple of deep breaths. Maybe I didn't even need to panic. He hadn't interviewed me. That could be my saving grace. I hadn't posed for any pictures. In fact, he might not even have my last name. I didn't advertise it, and all payments were made out to my business rather than to me. I couldn't remember if I'd even given it to Claire.

I picked up my phone and scrolled through the article. It was a good piece, making me like and relate to Dan and Janie Holmes despite the threat it posed to me. He'd talked to Janie and Dan about how much they looked forward to Harold Cartwright's birthday every year because it was like a big family reunion.

A picture of Dan and Janie, their cheeks mashed up together, came next. I could see the family resemblance. Dan had dark brown hair instead of Janie's blonde, but they had the same blue eyes, the same narrow nose, and the same impishness to their smile, even though stubble surrounded Dan's.

Seeing that smile on Janie's face, so different from when I'd last seen her, created a warm, bubbly feeling in my chest. I hadn't wanted credit for what I'd done, but it felt good to have done it. To have done something truly good after so many years of hearing how I never did anything right.

Alan continued the article with how, while Dan was trying to save Harold Cartwright's life, he hadn't realized his daughter's life was in jeopardy as well.

And then there I was. My face. Not just my truck.

I'd noticed the photographer milling about, but I'd assumed he'd only be taking pictures of the guests, not the hired help. I'd thought I'd managed to keep my back to him just in case.

I'd been wrong.

There I was, setting cupcakes onto my display, my cheeks still red from rushing back and forth. I'd been so distracted by what I was doing that I hadn't constantly watched for the photographer. Failure to pay attention was fatal error number one when it came to survival. It was what led to women being grabbed while out running alone, and it might hand me to Jarrod.

The picture wasn't a straight-on shot. A stranger wouldn't have been able to pick me out on the street from it. There was a chance Jarrod wouldn't recognize me, either. He'd liked my hair long and straight, and he hadn't been satisfied with my natural chestnut brown. He'd preferred I dyed my hair platinum. He'd also made sure I knew how haggard and old I looked without makeup on.

I hadn't purchased anything other than Chapstick since

making my break from him. I'd also chopped my hair up to my shoulders and dyed it black, letting my natural waves take care of the rest of the transformation. It'd been so long since he saw me with anything other than the look he liked that he might not know it was me if he saw the article in passing.

But haircuts and makeup, or the lack thereof, couldn't fool facial recognition software. Not even the fifteen pounds I'd lost from skipping meals could fool it. My bone structure and the spacing between my eyes and nose and lips hadn't changed.

Jarrod had made a point of telling me how it all worked so that, if I ever thought about leaving him, I'd know that he'd eventually find me.

What I didn't know was how often he'd run a check for me. Was it automated, or did he have to run it himself? If it was something he did manually, I might have a little time, a few weeks, since he was only one person and he wouldn't want to get caught. If it were automatic, I had until the weekend. He wouldn't risk leaving a trail, so he wouldn't take time off or fly. He'd drive roundtrip from Miami, Florida, stopping only long enough to kill me and dispose of my body. He'd be at work on time on Monday, with no one the wiser.

I slid out of the folding chair I set up in the back of my truck and went to the drawer where I kept all my paperwork. Claire Cartwright hadn't answered my calls any more than I'd answered Alan Brooksbank's. If I had enough money to change towns without what she owed me, I'd leave now.

Otherwise, I'd have to make a trip to visit Claire in person, insisting on being paid today, and then I'd head out of town and figure out where I was going next once I was on my way.

IF I HADN'T BEEN AFRAID OF BREAKING SOMETHING, I MIGHT HAVE slammed the drawer while putting my records away.

People might lie, but numbers don't, and the numbers said I couldn't afford to leave Lakeshore and start over without what Claire Cartwright owed me. I technically had enough to cover food and fuel while I relocated, even if I left Michigan entirely. What I didn't have was enough of a reserve to hold me over while I scoped out the best spots to set up on a daily basis and built a client base from the ground up—without any references, since I couldn't leave a trail from Lakeshore to my new location.

I also didn't have enough money in savings to change the name of my truck. At a minimum, I'd have to change my truck's name as soon as I set up someplace new. If Jarrod found my picture, he'd also have the name of my truck, making it that much easier for him to track me wherever I went. It'd be safer to repaint my whole rig, but I definitely didn't have enough money for that. Fortunately, the article never mentioned my assumed last name, calling me only Isabel, the owner/operator of the How Sweet It Is cupcake truck. At this point, anyway, I shouldn't need to buy a new identity.

I tried calling Claire one final time. It rang until her voice-mail picked up. Instead of leaving a message again, I hung up, climbed into the cab of my truck, and headed for her house. I needed what she owed me—now.

CHAPTER 5

An unsettling thought hit me as I drove to Claire Cartwright's. She might be intentionally avoiding me. She'd threatened to not pay the other food truck operator over fried onions and a lack of ketchup. Maybe she planned to withhold my payment because Harold collapsed before most of her guests had eaten my cupcakes.

I'd assumed she'd been too busy or grief-stricken to deal with the practicalities yet, and that was why she hadn't returned my calls.

That's because you're still too trusting, Fear whispered in my head. *You should know better by now. You can't trust anyone but yourself.*

At times like this, it was hard to decide whether Fear was right or wrong. If my dad were still alive, he'd tell me I shouldn't give my fear more power by personifying it in my imagination. He used to say that fear only existed to be conquered.

He'd never known Jarrod. Standing up for myself had only made things worse. Had it not been for Fear, I'd likely be dead already.

I pulled my truck over to the curb at the end of Claire's street. Her house was halfway down. Close enough for me to see her working outside in her front garden.

It seemed like a strange thing to be doing, planting flowers, when her grandfather had just died. In the weeks following my dad's death, I'd been too exhausted to do anything non-essential. I hadn't baked anything even though that was usually how I coped with stress. Some days, I hadn't even had the energy to eat.

But everyone reacted to grief differently.

I dialed Claire's number again.

The phone rang in my ear, and then she glanced down. She pulled a small rectangle that must be her phone off her waist. She looked at it and hooked it back onto her pants.

I disconnected the call before it went to voicemail again. There wasn't a point in leaving a message. She wasn't going to return my call no matter what I said on the message.

A normal businessperson would have been able to threaten sending her to collections or whatever people did when someone defaulted on what they owed. I couldn't even threaten it. I'd never follow through, and Claire seemed like the type of person who'd see right through any lie I'd tell her.

I didn't want any sort of confrontation with Claire. Just the thought of it sent tremors up my legs, and normally I'd have wanted a couple of weeks to rehearse what I'd say to her.

But I needed that money. The margin was too narrow without it, and if I couldn't afford to run my truck, I'd be on the street, vulnerable to more dangers than Jarrod.

I sucked in a breath to the count of three and let it out the same way. I had to do this. It wasn't like I was asking for something I wasn't owed, right? I'd spent the time and money on preparing the cupcakes. I'd delivered them as promised. I set them up.

That's what I'd tell her if she tried to argue that she shouldn't have to pay for cupcakes her guests didn't eat.

It wasn't as good an argument as I might have come up with if I had more time, and I wouldn't be able to prepare for any other arguments she might make, but it was what I had available.

I put my truck into drive and crawled down the street at a pace barely above what I would have used in an underground parking garage. I parked behind Claire's car in her driveway.

She looked up from her flower garden, and her expression shifted into one that looked like I'd tossed trash at her rather than simply parking my truck on her property. It couldn't be that big a breach of whatever etiquette rulebook she lived by for me to show up unannounced.

I put my hand on the door handle, but it was like trying to work a puppet that I couldn't see. My body didn't want to get out of my truck. It wanted me to put the truck back into reverse and leave, money or no money, rather than go out there with Claire glaring at me that way.

You also like to eat, I reminded my traitorous body. *And bake.*

I shoved the door open and hopped down. I'd read an article once about how body posture could make you feel braver, so I forced my shoulders back even though I'd much rather have hunched, making myself seem smaller.

"I tried to call," I said as I came around the front fender. I wanted her to know that I wouldn't have shown up uninvited if she'd answered my calls. I also needed to give her a way to save face. "But I think I must have the wrong number."

Claire didn't move from her spot beside the flower bed, either to meet me or to block my path. She didn't even pull her dirt-covered gloves off. "We both know you called the right number. I imagine you have my number programmed into your phone."

I stuttered to a stop one step from the line where her cement driveway met her lawn, where not even a single dandelion dared to grow. The sharp edge of her driveway felt like a barbed-wire fence.

I hadn't expected her to essentially admit to ignoring me. I had no answer for that. Maybe she hadn't called back because she was still grieving, and she considered my arrival a rude intrusion. She'd probably planned to pay me, but I'd rushed things.

I should have waited more patiently. Now all I'd managed to do was make her angry.

You couldn't have waited, I reminded myself. *That article put a spotlight on you that Jarrod might see.*

But that didn't fix the fact that I'd rubbed Claire's feathers the wrong way, as my dad liked to say in his funny way of mixing metaphors. A perturbed Claire was a Claire who wasn't going to be easily convinced to pay me today.

If there was one thing I was relatively good at, though—other than baking—it was soothing an angry person. I certainly had enough practice at it. If I could sometimes calm Jarrod down enough to avoid a beating, I could certainly smooth things over with Claire.

"You're right. I did dial the same number, so there was no way it could be the wrong number. I guess I was hoping I'd misdialed."

Her clenched jaw didn't release even a micro-inch. It was like my words hit her anger barrier and bounced right back. I could almost feel them smash into my chest, threatening to knock the air out of me.

"You shouldn't be here," she said.

I'd been right. It had to be about the fact that she felt I was rushing her after Harold's death. "I wanted to tell you how sorry I am about your grandfather. I—"

She held up her hand. "Coming to express condolences to me

won't convince anyone that you weren't part of this. You need to leave now."

That I wasn't part of it? Part of what?

She couldn't mean that I played a part in Harold's death, but there didn't seem to be anything else she could mean. "Why would I have wanted to hurt your grandfather?"

"I'm sure someone paid you to put the almond butter into the ketchup after I hired you to cater the party for us. You knew he was allergic. I told the police that when they asked me what I knew about you, so don't think you're going to get away with it. The only people there who weren't friends or family were you and the hotdog vendor."

My vision blurred slightly. If someone put almond butter into the ketchup, they really had wanted to kill Harold Cartwright. No store-bought ketchup that I knew of included almond butter on the list of ingredients, and I'd always been a label-reader because of all my dad's allergies.

My fingerprints were all over the ketchup bottles. Telling the truth wouldn't help me. Borrowing them for holding together my display while the glue dried could easily be an excuse I'd come up with to hide my real reason for taking the ketchup. I'd had unfettered access to them for plenty long enough to put almond butter into all of them. Claire would insist when questioned that she'd told me ahead of time I'd have to set up a proper display for the cupcakes. It'd look like I'd pretended to misunderstand in order to give myself an excuse to handle the ketchup.

"I hope whoever hired you paid you well," Claire was saying. "You won't get a penny from me."

Getting paid was suddenly the least of my concerns. If the newspaper article didn't lead Jarrod straight to me, a police investigation would. My prints were probably already in the system. They wouldn't come back to Isabel Addington. She didn't exist.

Amy Miller did. And her husband had promised to kill her if she ever tried to leave him.

Jarrod had been a lot of things, but one thing I knew about him—he always kept his promises.

I backed away from Claire. There was nothing I could say or do that would convince her of my innocence. Staying longer would only heighten her anger at me and make her more determined to see me convicted of Harold's murder.

I climbed into my truck and pulled out of Claire's driveway a little faster than I should have. Claire didn't chase after me or yell or anything as unseemly as that. She didn't have to. The look she sent after me said it all.

I was enemy number one. If Jarrod came looking for me, she'd not only believe whatever lies he told her about me, she'd point him right to me.

The problem was, I still didn't have the money to run. It

wouldn't do me any good to end up stranded somewhere because I couldn't afford to put gas in my truck.

My options for getting money any other way were slim. I'd do a lot of things to avoid Jarrod, but stealing wasn't one of them. I wouldn't hurt someone else to save myself. I also wouldn't sell my body.

I didn't have the time to pick up an outside job, even if I could get one without a social security number and references.

I drove to a park that I knew would be almost empty this time of day and shut off my truck. I wasn't safe to drive at the moment. The last thing I needed was to get into an accident and then have a warrant out for my arrest because I fled the scene.

Oh no.

I dropped my head forward onto my steering wheel. Even if I had what Claire owed me, I couldn't leave Lakeshore as long as I was a person of interest in a murder investigation.

Fleeing town would make me the prime suspect, and the police would issue a be-on-the-lookout for me and my truck. There'd be no explaining my way out of running, and I wouldn't be safe no matter where I went.

If Jarrod found me before the police did, he'd have a built-in reason to shoot me. I was a murder suspect, a clearly guilty one, who'd tried to escape. He'd warned me, and I didn't listen. He had no choice but to kill me.

I couldn't ditch my truck and my current name and start over, either. Buying a new identity and repainting a food truck took money. I might have enough to replace my name once more if I wasn't picky about where the new name came from, but not if I also wanted to rename my truck, too.

The life insurance my dad left me was the only money I'd had that Jarrod didn't control. After my dad died, I'd put it into an account, but I couldn't bear to touch it. I hadn't even told Jarrod about it when we married. I knew he'd say it was a waste not to use it. I'd finally emptied it to buy my truck and my name the first time.

I propped my chin on my steering wheel so I could see out the front windshield.

The wind had shifted, causing the waves to lap against the shore. My first night in Lakeshore, I'd walked this beach, picking up beach glass left behind by the storm the night before. I felt a lot like one of those pieces of glass. Broken. Tossed around by circumstances outside my control. Worn down.

They weren't what they once were, but they were still beautiful. Collecting a few of them had given me a little hope. Like maybe if I held on long enough, I'd make it through the storm, too.

I didn't know how long I could keep doing this.

For once, Fear didn't have an answer for me. He was telling me it wasn't safe to stay, and it wasn't safe to go.

Since I knew I had to go, the only thing I could do was to make leaving safe again.

To do that, I had to somehow show that I wasn't the one who killed Harold Cartwright.

And the only surefire way to do that was to prove someone else did.

It seemed unreal to consider investigating this crime. I'd always been an avid reader—a side effect of having a dad who taught English—but I'd never wished I could solve crimes like the sleuths I read about. I wasn't brilliant like Sherlock Holmes.

I didn't even have the skills of the real-life investigators I knew. I wasn't as good with people as Nicole Fitzhenry-Dawes, whose wedding I'd catered in the last town I'd stayed in.

I didn't see what other choice I had, though. I'd have to take whatever skills I did have and use them to figure out who killed Harold Cartwright.

And I had to do it fast. The longer I stayed in Lakeshore, the greater the chance that Jarrod would find me.

CHAPTER 6

All the way back to the farmer's market where I liked to park the truck to sleep, I chewed on the question of why someone would kill a hundred-year-old man. It seemed almost silly. At that age, it was a miracle that he woke up in the morning. All the person who killed him had to do was wait a little longer and the natural process of life would have done their job for them, without the risk of prison time.

There had to be a reason they couldn't wait. Maybe someone needed their inheritance? I couldn't think of any other reason to kill someone so old. Even revenge seemed unlikely. Anyone who wanted revenge would have taken it long ago, when it would have stung more for Harold to die.

As I pulled into the farmer's market, the parking lot was empty, as usual for a weekday. It only ran Friday to Sunday. But the back lock on the building didn't work, allowing me easy access to the bathrooms.

I parked my truck, went around to the back end, and set up my lawn chair so I wouldn't have to sit on the floor. I grabbed the paper and pencil I'd used to calculate my numbers, crossed them out, and wrote *MOTIVE* below. I added the word *inheritance*.

One motive was a pretty pathetic start, but I had to start somewhere.

So, working off the assumption that getting their inheritance was the motive, the people who'd be most likely to benefit from Harold's death were his immediate family.

I opened the Internet browser on my phone and searched for Harold Cartwright's obituary. Obituaries always listed the deceased's family.

His name came up alongside Ryder Funeral Home. I tapped the link.

His funeral wasn't until later this week. That seemed like a long time between death and internment, but the delay was probably due to the need for an autopsy since police believed he'd been murdered. They wouldn't have released the body to the funeral home until they felt they had all the evidence from it that they might need.

That also meant I still had time. The investigation was in its early stages. My name could be one of many, and they might not have started officially investigating me yet.

I scrolled down the page to read his obituary. It didn't list his cause of death, only that he'd passed away at the age of one hundred.

The paragraph listing his family members was one of the longest I'd seen. Harold Cartwright had six children, all of whom had married and produced grandchildren. He even had great-grandchildren. Any of them could be a suspect for an inheritance.

All I could do was start narrowing it down.

I followed the list, writing down the name of each person who hadn't predeceased Harold. It turned out he'd outlived three of his children.

Claire's name was listed as one of the grandchildren, but her name was given as Claire VanDyke, and her husband's name was in parentheses behind her name. Because she'd given her name as Claire Cartwright, I'd assumed Harold was actually her husband's grandfather. The Claire listed had to be her. She was the only Claire.

I tapped my pencil on the spot on my list where Claire's name would go. Claire didn't seem like someone who needed to murder for money. Her house was brick and had to be at least three or four bedrooms based on the size, and her car was newer than anything I'd ever owned before I married Jarrod.

But maybe the motive wasn't money. Claire had been very quick to want to point the finger at someone else, and she had been the one bringing Harold his food the day of the picnic, while he sat in a place of honor.

I wrote her name down even though my instincts told me Claire wasn't the one. Her anger at me had seemed too genuine.

Then again, I'd been played before.

I finished off the list. Dan Holmes—Janie's dad—was also on the list of grandchildren.

That one was surprising. Based on his picture, he was late thirties at best, and Claire was approaching sixty.

I put his name down, too, despite him seeming even less likely a suspect than Claire. If he'd put the almond butter into the ketchup, he wouldn't have let Janie eat any of it.

I set my phone aside. My list was eighteen people long. There was no way I'd have time to poke into all their lives. It'd be hard enough if I had only a single suspect.

My hand strayed to my phone as if it had a mind of its own. If I called Nicole—my former catering client who was the closest thing I had to a friend—she might have a suggestion about where to start. She'd also probably want to make the two-hour drive to Lakeshore to act as my legal counsel, just in case.

I couldn't have her doing that. Not only did I not want her finding out that I was still living in my truck, but I'd only talked to her once since I left Fair Haven. I always made sure not to leave any trails from one town to the next for Jarrod to follow. If Nicole knew where I was now, or worse, came to see me, it'd put her in danger. I refused to do that.

I pushed my phone away. For now, at least, I had to do this on my own. It was safer that way.

Which still left me with the problem of deciding where to start.

I ran my finger down the list. *Eenie meenee miney moe* didn't seem like a very logical or methodical way to approach it.

I needed to think, and the best way to clear my head had always been to bake something.

The carrot-cake cake pops I'd been forced into making because the cupcakes were destroyed had been a little too moist to hold together the way I wanted them to, but the flavor had been delicious. If I could get the ratio of icing to cake right, and maybe add a touch of something to the chocolate coating to give depth to the flavor, they'd be a great addition to my menu. A cake pop was easy for people who were on the move to buy and eat while they went. It'd also be a frugal use of the cupcakes that didn't sell each day. If I turned them into cake pops, I wouldn't have to reduce their price as day-olds.

I pulled the leftover ones I'd baked for yesterday out of my fridge and scraped the icing off into a bowl.

With the ones I'd salvaged for Harold's party, I hadn't had the luxury of experimenting with the cake-to-icing ratio. I'd dumped it all together into a bowl and hoped for the best.

I froze with a cupcake in one hand. I hadn't had a chance to experiment in part because of what happened to the cupcakes when the man smashed into me in the parking lot.

The man had seemed nervous, like he wanted to get as far away from the party as possible. He might have somehow put the almond butter into the ketchup and then wanted to get away before Harold ate it.

He'd looked too young to be Harold's grandchild, but given the gap in age between Claire Cartwright and Dan Holmes, it was possible.

I set aside my cupcakes and picked up my phone and list again. I typed each male grandchild's name—except Dan Holmes, since I knew what he looked like—into my search bar one at a time. About half of them had a professional page or social media account that showed a public picture. None of them were the man who'd run into me.

It'd been hoping for too much that finding out his identity would be that easy. I tossed my phone and pad of paper back into my chair.

I pulled on latex gloves and broke the cupcakes up into a bowl. The problem with my theory was that, without a name, it wasn't enough to take to the police. I had a random guess at a motive. If I went to the police and told them about a nameless man who bumped into me in the parking lot, it'd only make me look guiltier. It'd sound like I made him up to throw suspicion off myself. They'd end up investigating me more closely, which was exactly what I hoped to avoid.

What I needed was a name and a solid motive. Then I could take it to the police without seeming questionable, and they could take it from there. Once their attention was directed toward him, I should be able to leave town without arousing suspicion.

But that left me with a catch-twenty-two. I couldn't find him because I didn't know his name, and I couldn't find out his name because I didn't know how to find him. It made the blood pound behind my eyes just thinking of it.

I measured out how much cake I had, measured some icing, and dumped it together. I gave the mixture a few exuberant squishes, and my blood pressure dropped.

Baking really was better than therapy. You didn't have to bare your soul to anyone, and you ended up with something delicious to eat afterward. It was a win-win.

Unfortunately, baking wouldn't help me find my mystery man.

The fact that he'd been trying to leave before Harold ate the ketchup might mean he had some sense of guilt for what he'd done. It could also just mean he thought leaving would give him a better alibi since he wasn't around when it happened, but I didn't think so. He'd been smart enough to come up with putting an allergen into a safe food item, so he had to realize the police would know that could have been done at any time. The killer didn't have to be around when Harold ate the tainted ketchup.

Leaving suggested that he didn't have the heart to watch it happen.

Logically, then, he might show up at the funeral as an act of penitence. Even if he wasn't remorseful, if I was right and he was a grandchild, it'd look strange to everyone if he didn't attend the funeral.

Attending the funeral as well seemed like my best chance to find out who he was. I'd recognize him if I saw him again, and all I'd have to do was introduce myself to him under the guise of expressing my condolences. None of the grandchildren had the same first name, so if he matched one of the first names, I'd have his last name as well.

My plan sounded great in theory, but in practice I'd have a major obstacle. I had to do all of that without Claire spotting me.

CHAPTER 7

The best word I could think of to describe the church where Harold Cartwright's funeral was being held was quaint—and I meant it in its flattering sense. The building was sided in white clapboard and topped with an impossibly skinny steeple that looked like it couldn't be strong enough to support the giant bronze bell at the top.

I didn't sign the guestbook on the way in, nor did I take one of the bulletins. Doing either of those things would have been disrespectful to the actual mourners. It was bad enough I'd be taking up a seat. Had it not been for the fact that I didn't want to make myself easier for Claire to spot, I would have chosen to stand and allowed someone else to sit.

All the pews were already filled with so many people they sat with their arms touching. Based on the number of pews and size of the sanctuary, the church could probably comfortably accommodate a hundred and fifty people. The church had to be filled well past the amount allowed by the fire marshal.

Extra chairs lined the wall behind the final pew. I slid into one of the few remaining seats. Before the service had a chance to start, people were standing along the wall.

My dad's funeral had been much smaller. He'd been an only child, and he'd had to quit teaching before I was even out of high school because of his heart.

But my mailman must have put his back out carrying all the condolence cards I received from former students who'd learned of my dad's passing. It'd helped a little to know I wasn't the only one who would miss him.

I craned my neck to check out the pews reserved for family at the front. The back of Claire's head looked like she'd recently had her hair cut and styled. Unless her husband also dyed his hair, he couldn't be the man sitting beside her. The hair of the man beside her was much too dark, and the blonde child beside him made me think it might be Dan Holmes.

There were a few men with the same blond hair as the man who ran into me in the parking lot in the front pews, but until I saw their faces, I couldn't be sure if the one I was looking for was there or not.

The pianist hit the notes of the first hymn, and the minister invited everyone to stand. My legs responded instinctively, my years growing up in the church coming back to me.

I let the music flow around me. It felt as though it drew the tension out of my body like a poultice draws out an infection. I almost felt like that little girl again—the one who used to snuggle into her daddy's side, sucking on the caramel-flavored candies he kept in his suit pockets, special for church.

A church was the one place I knew Jarrod wouldn't look for me. He'd been almost militant in his atheism, mocking people of faith as stupid and taking every opportunity to point out when one of them was caught in hypocrisy. I'd been so angry at God over my dad's death when I met Jarrod that I'd gone along with whatever he said.

It was why, when I'd decided to try to leave, I'd walked the two miles to the nearest church on a Sunday morning while Jarrod was at the golf course. It was less than a week after losing my baby. I'd finally realized it was only a matter of time until he killed me, too. And I wasn't ready to die.

Walking away isn't as easy as some people think, even when you want to. I didn't have a car. I didn't have any friends left to call. Even if I had, he had my cell phone linked to his somehow so he knew everywhere I went and everyone I called. He'd know who helped me, and he'd find me. I'd had to figure out a way to get help that he couldn't trace.

That Sunday, I left my cell phone under the bed, packed what I could into a backpack, and went straight into the pastor's office while he was preparing for the service. I told him I needed help leaving my husband.

The *why don't we make an appointment to talk about this* and *we can set you and your husband up with a Christian counsellor* stopped as soon as I pulled up my shirt and showed him the bruises across my belly.

"Do you want me to call the police for you?" he'd asked. "You should report this."

"My husband *is* the police," I replied.

While the pastor preached his sermon, his wife drove me to a women's shelter two towns away in the hope that it would make it harder for Jarrod to find me. The next day, I emptied out the one bank account Jarrod and I hadn't shared—the one that contained my dad's life insurance.

Even though I wasn't sure what I believed about God anymore, standing in a church still soothed my nerves. That probably made me morbid since I was here for a funeral, trying to catch a murderer, but the truth was the truth. A church felt safe to me, like a haven, regardless of why I was there.

The minister gave an overview of Harold's life that made me wish I'd gotten to know him. It also left me even more confused about why someone would have wanted to end his life early. It had to be for money.

Of course, funerals were a lot like movie trailers—showing you the highlights. Behind the scenes, he could have been a mean drunk, and you'd never know about it from attending his funeral. No one knew what Jarrod did to me behind closed doors.

The minister invited anyone who wished to go to the cemetery for the internment and then meet back in the basement of the church for the luncheon.

I straightened in my seat, ready to get up. Now was my chance. The pallbearers would take the coffin out to the hearse, and the family would file out afterward, giving me the perfect opportunity to see if the man from the parking lot was here. I could melt into the crowd of departing people right alongside him.

Six men from the front pews rose and headed for the coffin—the pallbearers.

They took their place and turned around to face the congregation.

My heart felt like it slammed into the underside of my ribcage.

The pallbearer on the other side of the coffin from Dan Holmes was the man who'd run into me in the parking lot. My odds of being right about who killed Harold when up in equal proportion to how my chances of actually getting to him in time to find out his name went down. Unless I sprinted out of the church now, in front of the casket—which would draw the attention of everyone in the place—I'd have to have the speed of Superman to catch him.

That didn't mean I wasn't going to try, though. While I might be able to find him at the gravesite or at the luncheon after, doing either of those increased my chances of Claire spotting me. I wasn't entirely sure she wouldn't call the police on me if she saw me here.

The casket passed by, and I shifted to the edge of my seat. I glanced up to watch for the first person who looked like they weren't immediate family to make their move so I could make mine.

My gaze met Claire's.

The old cliché talks about a person's eyes shooting daggers. Claire's eyes shot harpoons, pinning me to my chair.

Not good.

I hunched down, but she held eye contact. She passed within five feet of me, and only looked away when she reached the point that she would have had to walk backward to keep watching me.

I needed to get the man's name and get out of here fast. Even more than I didn't want to cause a scene, I didn't want to cause a scene at a funeral.

The problem was that Claire would likely stop beside the hearse to watch Harold's casket being loaded. If I tried to approach the man now, I'd be heading straight for her.

My only recourse seemed to be to try to blend into the crowd. It increased the risk of the man disappearing before I could catch him, but I wouldn't catch him anyway if Claire cornered me.

I didn't wait for anyone else to pass by. I got to my feet and eased into the moving crowd, letting the natural momentum carry me forward. I edged to the right. If I could come out of the church on the opposite side of the doors from where I'd been sitting, I'd be between the hearse and the parking lot. That should mean the young man would have to pass by me to reach his car and that I'd be separated from Claire by enough people that she'd lose track of me.

I exited the door. The entrance went down four steps. From the top, I had a view of everything below. The funeral home's employee slammed the door on the back of the hearse. The blond man was already on the fringe of the crowd, heading toward the parking lot.

And Claire was leaning close to Dan. She pointed up at me.

That couldn't be good in any scenario.

Maybe I shouldn't have left Fair Haven. It wasn't safe, but Lakeshore wasn't safe anymore, either. At least in Fair Haven, people had believed me when I said I didn't kill anyone, and I'd had someone who wanted to call me a friend.

Of course, that was exactly why it'd been necessary for me to leave. The only thing worse than Jarrod killing me would be Jarrod killing someone else because of me.

I strode down the stairs in the direction of the parking lot, trying to look like I was simply heading for a car, even though my truck was parked two blocks away. If they thought I was leaving, they might let me go.

And I might still be able to get the man's name if I could catch up to him. I'd get his name and keep on walking.

He stepped over the curb into the parking lot, and I lengthened my stride.

"Excuse me," a man's voice called from behind me. "Ma'am?"

It was probably Dan calling for me, but since I didn't know that for sure, it gave me plausible deniability.

I kept walking. The man ahead of me raised his hand slightly in a gesture I recognized as him pressing his car clicker. A tan SUV's back lights flashed one row in front of us.

"Ma'am?" The voice was closer now.

A hand brushed my shoulder. I cringed to the side and spun around.

Dan Holmes stood behind me. He must have stepped back after I'd flinched from his touch because he now stood far enough away that an outstretched hand wouldn't make contact with me.

A small feather of grudging respect tickled my heart. He could have sensed my fear and closed in like a predator stalking wounded prey. Given what Claire had probably told him, that's what I would have expected. Intimidate me. Scare me. Threaten me.

He hadn't. Instead, he'd given me some space, trying to make sure I didn't flee.

He smiled in a way that most women would have found

disarming. I'd learned my lesson about being lulled into a false security by a handsome face—and Dan Holmes was exactly the kind of man I tended to find appealing, with his dark hair, stubble, and broad shoulders—but that smile did make me feel ten years younger and a lot prettier than I knew I was.

"I didn't mean to startle you," he said. "You're the cupcake lady from Grandpa's birthday, aren't you?"

As if he didn't know. "That was me."

"Isabel…"

He let my name drag out so that I could hear the question mark on the end. He wanted me to supply my last name.

A car engine started behind me, and I glanced back over my shoulder. Oh no. The tan SUV. I'd missed my chance.

He backed out of his parking spot, moving closer to where we stood. I could easily read his Michigan license plate—C8L 364D. I currently had no way to figure out who a license plate belonged to, but it was better than nothing. Assuming I could remember the correct plate number.

I turned back to Dan and gave him a return smile that I hoped looked natural. What had he said before I got distracted? Right, he'd been fishing for my last name. "Isabel of How Sweet It Is Cupcake Truck."

It felt like a situation where I should offer to shake his hand, but his hands were so big. If he got a hold of me and refused to let go, I wouldn't be strong enough to break away.

He gave me another smile that made me think he recognized my dodge but was too much of a gentleman to call me on it. It was a smile with a laugh behind it, and it made his eyes crinkle at the corners, something I couldn't help but find endearing.

"My cousin pointed you out to me, and I wanted to thank you for what you did for Janie."

This conversation wasn't going how I'd expected so far. Maybe that's why Claire sent him instead of coming herself. He was cagier—the lock pick to her stick of dynamite. I was sure Claire hadn't actually been pointing me out because I saved Janie.

I repeated the license plate number over to myself, but it was going to be hard to keep it straight if he held me here for long. I needed to make it memorable somehow.

Sherlock Holmes would have used a mind palace, but the only place I knew well enough for that was my truck. It wasn't big enough to walk through a license plate number. Making up a silly story might work though.

Like Claire eating lice for 364 days...because of course she wouldn't eat regular old lice on Christmas.

I fought back a grin. My thought life was the one thing no one else could control. That said, I didn't need Dan thinking my smirk had something to do with the horrible situation at Harold's birthday party.

"I recognized the signs." I took a step backward. Maybe he'd let me leave if I moved away slowly. "I'm glad I was in the right place at the right time."

Dan moved forward as if he were going to walk along with me if I decided to try to leave. "With everyone else clustered around Grandpa, we might not have seen her in time. To have someone there who wasn't distracted by what was happening and who understands allergies was a blessing."

That slight smile was still on his face, but there was something in the way he held my gaze that made me think his words meant more than it seemed on the surface.

Like he thought it was more than a fortunate coincidence. Like he was really asking why I hadn't also been distracted by Harold's collapse. Like he was wondering whether my knowledge of allergic reactions came because I'd been hired to make sure Harold suffered one.

Even contract killers probably had a line they wouldn't cross. Maybe he thought mine was killing innocent children by accident. It wasn't an implausible explanation for what had happened. My rescue of Janie had probably been the one thing Claire hadn't been able to make fit into her story that I'd been behind Harold's death.

It was strange, standing there facing him, because, unlike with Claire, I felt like he actually wanted me to be able to provide a good reason. He wanted me to be innocent and uninvolved.

The pull of having someone believe me was too strong. I stopped my backward momentum. "My dad died from a wasp sting."

"I'm sorry to hear that," Dan said, and I believed him.

People were now flowing around us on their way to their cars.

Dan motioned back to where the hearse still waited at the curb. "Are you staying for the luncheon?"

I shook my head. "I have to get back to work."

"Thanks for coming. And for what you did for Janie."

He turned around and strode away. His arms swung at his sides in a way that spoke of a calm and confidence that some people seemed born with.

A cold pinprick feeling skittered over the back of my neck and down my arms. Why did it feel like I'd just given something away? Did he plan to use the information about my dad to try to figure out my last name?

I was probably being overly paranoid again. Everything Dan had said or done might have been for exactly the reason he'd given—I'd saved his daughter's life and he wanted to thank me.

But it'd felt like it could be fishing for information.

Each year in the U.S., fifty-eight people died from bee, wasp, and hornet stings. I'd looked it up after my dad died. Dan might be able to find a list of those people somewhere, but he didn't know when my dad died. It'd be easy for him to guess that I was in my thirties, but he'd still have well over two thousand people to look at if he tried to make a list. Even assuming half those people were women, it'd take him a lot longer to look up over a thousand people to see if they had a daughter named Isabel than I planned to be in Lakeshore.

By the time he figured out that he couldn't find me that way, I'd be long gone.

Or at least, I would be if I could figure out a way to match the license plate number I'd gotten with a name.

CHAPTER 8

Two days passed and I still hadn't yet figured out how to identify who a license plate belonged to. It looked like that information wasn't available to just any member of the public. Private investigators might be able to access a database, but I definitely couldn't afford to hire a PI.

On the positive side, my carrot cake pops sold out both days. One of the women who'd become a regular told me carrot cake was her favorite, but she'd never bought my carrot cake cupcakes in the past because of the nuts. Her building had a nut-free policy. The daycare center in the building had some children with severe nut allergies, and management had decided it wasn't worth the risk to even have nuts in the building.

She said she was going to recommend me to cater meetings instead of the baskets of dry muffins they'd been bringing in. She'd seen the article on me in the paper and thought it would win me the contract. I clearly understood how dangerous allergies could be. Too many food places didn't. One time they'd brought in clients and had nothing for them because the bakery they'd ordered from sent brownies with walnuts in them.

Instead of telling her I wasn't likely to be around past next week, I handed her my card. If I could cater even a meeting or two before I left, it'd help my flagging bank account.

After fifteen minutes without another customer, I figured the lunch crowd was back to work.

I pulled the mostly empty displays off the counter and dropped my flap. I stepped outside and clicked the locks into place. My hope had been to commission a painted sign I could snap to the top of the truck when I set up someplace for more than a few hours. It'd catch attention better and be easier for people to read from a distance than the words painted on my truck. That would have to wait as well.

I closed my eyes and turned my face up to the sun for a moment. Michigan was finally starting to feel as warm as a Florida winter. It was beautiful sports weather. The online local newspaper said the boy's high school baseball team from Lakeshore's biggest high school was playing their archrivals tonight. I'd called the school secretary this morning, and she'd told me food trucks were allowed as long as we parked in the one small area designated for vendors and didn't take up parking meant for spectators.

I planned to head straight there now, even though the game

was still hours away, to make sure I got a spot. From what I'd read in the paper about previous games, the boy's ball team was on a hot streak, and the stands should be packed.

My cell phone rang, and I jumped. It'd been stupid and indulgent of me to close my eyes that way. Jarrod could have sneaked up on me, and I wouldn't have seen him coming.

I climbed back into my truck and grabbed my cell phone on the last ring before it would have funneled the call to my voicemail.

"This is Alan Brooksbank," a man's voice said, "the Positivity Project columnist."

It wasn't lost on me that he made sure to tell me what he wrote this time. Like I could forget. Had I had enough time to look at the phone before I answered, I might not have picked up.

Though it wasn't like he could do much more damage to me now.

I also couldn't think of anything to say to him other than *Do you have any idea of the problems you've created?* And I certainly couldn't say that. Or how tired I was of running. Or how what I wanted more than almost anything was to sleep for a few nights on a real mattress. To think I used to like camping as a kid.

Instead of saying any of that, I let the silence stretch.

"Anyway," Alan said, with a nervous edge to his voice that hadn't been there before, "I know physical newspapers seem to be going the way of the cassette tape these days, but the paper still likes to give complimentary copies to anyone when we do a story on them. I was hoping I'd be able to drop your copies off to you sometime this afternoon."

Okay, that wasn't such a bad thing. Maybe I could frame a copy and hang it up by my menu for people to read while they were waiting for their cupcake. It certainly couldn't hurt.

I felt like a balloon of optimism had been inflating in my chest and was popped. That wouldn't work. I had to change my truck's name as soon as I left Lakeshore. I was already taking a big risk not leaving the business behind entirely. But I loved baking too much to walk away yet. If I let Jarrod steal everything I enjoyed from me, was my life even worth living?

If I was going to give up baking, I might as well let the police arrest me for Harold's murder and lock me away. At least I'd be safe from Jarrod in prison, I wouldn't have to worry about whether I'd have enough to eat, and I'd have a real bed to sleep on.

It was looking like that would be my fate anyway since I had no way to prove my theory about the man who ran into me in the parking lot the day Harold Cartwright died.

"Isabel?" Alan asked. "Are you still there?"

I leaned back against my fridge and looked at my phone. It was a long shot, but maybe a reporter would have a way to find out who belonged to a license plate. That seemed like something a reporter might need to do for an undercover story. Those weren't the kind of stories Alan wrote, but that didn't mean he didn't have contacts.

"I'm still here."

The problem was, I couldn't tell him why I needed to know who the license plate belonged to. That would require telling him information about myself that I wasn't comfortable sharing, and he probably wouldn't want to get in the middle of a police investigation in any way.

"I have a favor to ask, actually," I said to make sure he didn't end the call.

I had to think quick. He wrote the Positivity Project, so he was a sucker for happy-ending, do-gooder stories.

"I clipped the mirror on a car the other day. I didn't have a paper and pen to leave my name, and I couldn't wait around because I was on my way to a job. I took a picture of the license plate, thinking I could find the owner that way. I didn't realize that information wasn't available to everyone. If I texted you the number, do you have any resources to help me find the car's owner so I can make it right?"

I clamped my mouth shut before I could ramble on. Over-explaining was one of the biggest red flags that a person was lying—or at least, that's what Jarrod had told me. While he wasn't the best example of a human being, he was good at his job.

It was Alan's turn to go quiet. In the background, I could

hear music playing. I didn't recognize the song, but it had a beat that made me want to hum to it.

"I've never needed to check a license plate before." His words were slow, as if he were picking them with care. "I'll see if anyone has any connections who could make it happen, but I can't promise you."

An *I'll try* was better than where I stood now. "I appreciate you trying."

"Can we set up a time to meet? I'll give you the copies of my story and the owner's name and number…if I can get it."

Why is he so insistent on meeting you? Fear whispered in my ear.

It'd been difficult enough for me to accept catering jobs from clients because Fear had told me those were perfect opportunities for Jarrod to know exactly where I'd be. I'd had to do those because catering jobs were a food truck's bread and butter—or, in my case, cake and icing.

This was different. For all I knew, Jarrod had contacted Alan and asked him to lure me to some location. Jarrod wouldn't have told Alan who he really was or who I really was. There'd have been some convincing tale behind it, like he'd seen Alan's article and recognized his long-lost sister. Could Alan arrange a surprise meeting? Someone like Alan Brooksbank would jump on a follow-up story chance like that. He'd never suspect Jarrod's motives weren't genuine.

I couldn't take that risk.

"I'll pop by the newspaper's office sometime early next week." My phone beeped in my ear, letting me know I had another call coming in. Saved by the beep. "I have another call. I'll see you then."

I switched over before Alan could argue and answered with my practiced *This is Isabel of How Sweet It Is Cupcake Truck.*

"I'm glad I caught you before you closed for the day," another male voice said.

The voice was vaguely familiar, but I couldn't quite place it. It was deeper than Jarrod's. I was sure I'd have recognized his voice even if he tried to disguise it. It also had a slower, more relaxed cadence to it than Alan's. Alan's voice carried that upbeat pace of someone who was naturally energetic or had drunk too many caffeinated beverages in a short period of time.

I slid into the driver's seat of my truck, but I didn't start the engine. I'd hooked up my phone to Bluetooth so I could always answer while driving. That would send my call through the truck, which tended to slightly distort the voice on the other end and make it harder for me to pinpoint the speaker. He hadn't identified himself. My regular clients usually gave their names right away.

Maybe he wasn't someone I knew. Many people had similar voices.

"How can I help you?" I asked.

"I'm hoping you cater small events. My daughter has a big role in her school's end-of-the-year play, and every family is supposed to bring a dessert for the party afterward. I don't know how to bake."

The way he said it all took a bit of the stiffness out of my shoulders. His tone wasn't so self-deprecating as to suggest he had low self-esteem, but it also wasn't the cocky tone some men had where they seemed to think not knowing how to cook or bake was a manly badge of honor. His tone was more like *I know I should learn, but help me out of a bind for now.*

"I do small events, and I also do orders for pickup." As much as I could use the money, this dad sounded like a decent guy who was trying to make sure he didn't embarrass his kid. I didn't want to take advantage of him. "It can be a bit pricy, though, compared to a bigger order. If you want a small order of something that's not already on my menu for that day, it means making a separate small batch. That's more time-consuming for me as a baker. Are you sure you wouldn't rather grab something from the grocery store?"

"Yeah, I thought of that, but I don't want to take the risk. My daughter has food allergies. I want to make sure there's something there I know she can safely eat. Her class had a picnic earlier this year, and she almost ate a brownie with nuts in it because someone forgot and didn't label them properly. I'd be happy to take a selection of what you already plan to prepare for that day."

After what I'd seen lately, I didn't blame him for being extra cautious. Most schools were trying to protect students with food allergies, but not every parent with non-allergic children understood the potential severity of it. Or would always remember. I'd read a sad story about a month ago about a child who died because he traded snacks with another kid in his class. The other kid's mom was facing a lawsuit from the dead child's family, but in the interview I'd read, she insisted she'd sent that food for her own child—who wasn't allergic—and she shouldn't be held responsible for the fact that some other child liked her child's food better than his own.

The clock on my dashboard flipped over to a new hour. This guy probably just sounded like someone I knew, and I needed to get to the school or I'd lose my chance at a space. I started my engine, let my phone switch over to Bluetooth, and walked him through how I preferred payment, my cancellation policy, and all the usual details.

"I really appreciate it." His voice faded out, then came back in like he'd switched the phone from one ear to another. "I didn't have any allergies growing up, and I didn't realize how hard it would be. I want to make sure she has a normal childhood and doesn't feel left out."

Switching his phone from one side to the other struck me as odd. It was something you did when you either planned to continue talking for a while longer or you needed your dominant hand free to write something down. Since the conversation was almost over, I guessed the latter. He should have done that before I started giving him details about what I'd need to know from him, not after. It meant he hadn't written down what I'd said, but he was preparing to write something down.

"So," he said, "all I still need from you then is your last name so the school can do a background check. They require it for all volunteers."

I felt a click in my brain that reminded me of a stuck key finally turning in a lock. I did know the man's voice. It was Dan Holmes.

I almost sent up a prayer of thanks that I hadn't fallen for it completely. I might very well have given him my last name. He'd have taken it to the police, and they would have discovered quickly that I had to be operating under a false name. While that alone wasn't a crime—though possessing the fake ID I carried was—it would make me their primary suspect in Harold's death.

If they brought me in for questioning, I'd have no choice but to give them my real name and show them my real ID. Giving them the fake ones meant a guaranteed possession charge, bringing with it fines or jail time.

Of course, giving them my real name meant giving Jarrod proof positive of where I was. While he might think twice about making the trip across the country over a photo that might or might not be me, he wouldn't hesitate a second if my name popped up in the system.

But bluntly refusing to give Dan my name without a reason also presented a problem—it'd only make him more suspicious.

Since he didn't know that I knew who he was, I might be able to dodge it in a believable way.

One thing I would have to thank Jarrod for when he finally caught me was that living with him had taught me how to talk my way out of things. Having a believable explanation at the ready had saved me more than once from a beating.

"You don't need to make the school go to all that trouble." I made sure to smile even though I didn't feel like it. I was convinced people could hear a smile in someone's voice even over the phone. "I'm not actually going to be a volunteer. I won't have any contact with the kids. I'll just drop the cupcakes off to you ahead of time. That way the other parents won't know you bought them."

He hummed like he was thinking about it. "That's tempting to help me save face, but I want to be able to focus on helping my daughter get ready. Getting her hair done right will be enough of a challenge without having to remember the cupcakes, too. I'd rather you set them up at the school."

Dan Holmes had an answer for everything I tried. It was like trying to best a grand master in a game of chess, even though I couldn't even name all the pieces. "Honestly, there's nothing to set up. When I'm not catering, I deliver them in a nice box, but that's it. You just have to open it and set it on the table."

His pause was long enough to let me know that he was trying to come up with some other reason I needed to give him my name. "You're probably right." He laughed, and if I hadn't known better, I would have thought it was genuine. "This is my first school play. I think I'm more nervous than she is. I'll get back to you with the exact date and the amount I'll need."

He ended the call. I drove my truck through the most circuitous route possible while still making sure to arrive at the high school early enough. It wasn't really necessary. Dan Holmes had no reason to be physically tailing me at this point. After a few turns, I was sure no one was following me.

But the shivers running over my skin wouldn't settle down. I wouldn't hear from him again about buying cupcakes from me, but I knew one thing for sure.

It wasn't only the police or Jarrod I needed to watch out for. Dan Holmes was determined to expose my secret and see me investigated for the death of Harold Cartwright.

CHAPTER 9

After the baseball game finished on Friday night, I drove my truck to an open but practically abandoned campground one town over and hid there until Monday.

Hiding out for the weekend leveled another blow to my bank account since weekends tended to earn me as much as I made during the whole rest of the week. But it was the only way I could make sure Jarrod wouldn't find me. He'd only have the weekend to be able to hunt for me without his absence being noted. By hiding away, I bought myself another week of safety.

I hoped.

A lot could have changed in the year I'd been gone. It was always possible that Jarrod had gone back to field work rather than the desk job he'd had for the past few years thanks to a promotion. If he'd gone back to field work, no days were safe. His "weekends" would be completely random.

I pushed the thought from my mind. There were too many *if*s. I couldn't try to counteract them all. I'd end up frozen.

On Monday, I kept my regular lunch spot—partly for the money, partly because my regulars counted on me to be there, and partly to give Alan as much time as possible to get me a name to go along with the license plate. As soon as the lunch crowd died off, I closed up and headed for the newspaper office.

I'd equipped my truck with a GPS, but I only used it when I first came to a town. Anywhere that I planned to stay for longer than a week, I studied an online map and memorized as much as I could. It wasn't that hard. I'd always loved the paper maps my dad and I used when we took vacations when I was a kid, before GPS was a thing. A GPS wouldn't help me if I were being followed. If someone were following me, my ability to escape could depend on how well I knew the roads and alternate routes.

It was especially true in Lakeshore. Whoever designed the roads had obviously been a masochist. The downtown and most of the business sectors were riddled with one-way streets. One of my earliest clients had told me the running joke among the locals was that the engineer who'd laid out their streets made them that way to encourage the tourists to walk rather than drive in the hope that they'd buy more if they were right next to the shop windows.

From what I'd seen of Lakeshore's shops, tourists would buy

regardless of whether they were on foot or had to park a car. The shops were some of the most interesting I'd ever seen, from Humblebee, selling all things beeswax from lip balm to candles, to Prism, filled with some of the most stunning glass artistry anywhere, to Just Beachy, a shop devoted entirely to signs, blankets, t-shirts, and pillows all declaring in some form how life was better at the beach.

One of my regrets was that I didn't have the time or the money to explore them all myself.

I parked my truck behind the bank next to the newspaper office because the bank's parking lot was the only place on the street with two exits. If I needed to make a getaway because this was a trap set by Jarrod, I'd have an easier time getting out.

The directory in the building's front lobby told me the newspaper office was on the second floor. I skipped the elevator and took the stairs.

The door for the newspaper office was a clear glass door with letters embossed on it, making it look a bit like a private detective's office from old black-and-white movies. Inside, about fifteen men and women moved around a room filled with metal desks. Flimsy cubical-style walls blocked the rest of the room off from the front, maybe separating the editorial staff from the regular reporters.

I pushed the door open, and the noise of the room hit me first—soft tapping from keyboards, voices, and the hum of electronics and fans.

I stopped a few steps inside. Surprising Alan Brooksbank had felt safer, but it also left me with a problem. I didn't have an appointment, so he wasn't watching for me, and I didn't know what he looked like.

A man in a wheelchair rolled to a stop beside me. "May I help you?"

I did a double take. The man's voice sounded enough like Alan's that it seemed improbable it wasn't him. But he was in a wheelchair. And he wasn't fresh out of college.

The man in front of me was in his early forties, with a shaved head and bulky shoulders and arm muscles straining at his dark t-shirt. He looked nothing like the image I'd had in my mind.

I realized I was staring just barely in time to answer his question before the pause got awkward. "I'm Isabel."

Alan smiled, his thin, wide lips reminding me a bit of the Grinch once his heart grew three sizes. It was a nice smile, just a little too big for his face. "Sorry about that. That picture I got wasn't clear enough for me to recognize you. And I expected you to stand me up. You sounded even more annoyed with me for calling about complimentary copies than you did when I asked you for the story in the first place."

If I'd been a cartoon character, my ears probably would have burst into little embarrassed flames. After all my years of hiding my true emotions from Jarrod, I should have been better at faking it. Though perhaps Alan saw through it because he was a reporter. They probably had to get good at reading interview subjects so they knew when to push and when not to.

Alan waved for me to follow him. "My desk's this way."

He weaved through the maze of desks with me trailing behind him. The spacing between the desks seemed to have been set up specifically to allow Alan enough room to maneuver, suggesting his condition wasn't a new one and that he was a valued member of the news team.

It didn't make sense. As much as I loved the Positivity Project, it'd always seemed to me like it was written by someone who hadn't seen the harsh realities of the world. Alan was in a wheelchair. He had to have some knowledge of how brutal and unfair life could be.

Alan pulled up to a desk nestled in next to the wall. The desk's owner had attached a large corkboard to the wall and filled it with pictures and letters, presumably from people who'd loved his writing.

Alan shifted a stack of handwritten pages to the side, revealing a couple neatly folded newspapers. "We used to give out five complementary copies, but now it's only two. The owners figured people could always print more off from our website if they wanted them." He passed the newspapers into my limp grip, wheeled himself around to the other side of the desk, and fished around in his drawer. "And I have the other information we talked about. As my way of apologizing since I get the feeling you'd rather I hadn't written the article at all."

That was an understatement, but it made me feel uncomfortable, like having a mosquito buzzing in my ear, to think I'd been that easy for anyone to read, even a trained reporter. At the time, I'd been more concerned about stopping the story than about revealing that I wanted to stop the story.

He straightened up, a yellow sticky note in his hand.

Despite his claim to have gotten it for me as an apology, he didn't immediately hand it over. His hesitation made me think he was considering holding it ransom for an explanation. His reporter's nose must be twitching at the scent of a deeper story. Why wouldn't a business person want publicity—especially good publicity—for their business? Good press meant more clients, after all.

I moved close enough that he could easily hand me the paper. "Humility was a virtue in my family growing up. I'm not comfortable with being in the spotlight."

He passed me the paper. "Humility sometimes brings honor. You saved that family from a double tragedy, and you deserved to be recognized for it."

His statement about humility reminded me vaguely of a Bible verse. My dad always had a Bible verse for everything. Hearing one, or something like one, quoted now brought a little sting to my heart. Not only because it was harder being on my own without any family or friends than I'd ever expected it to be, but also because Alan Brooksbank seemed to be the only one who believed I was a hero and not a villain.

I stuffed the sticky note into my pocket before he could decide to ask for it back, thanked him for the newspapers, and made my escape. The sooner I was alone, the sooner I could see if the name Alan got for me matched the name of one of Harold Cartwright's grandchildren.

CHAPTER 10

Deciphering Alan's doctor-level chicken scrawl after I'd gotten back to one of my safe spots took me almost ten minutes. Once I got most of the letters figured out, only one name on the list came close to matching—Blake Cartwright.

I drummed my fingers on my knees in my cross-legged position on my truck floor. Now I had a name—and a phone number, thanks to Alan—but I still didn't have a concrete motive to give to the police. Without that, he wouldn't bump to the top of the list.

I had to do a little more digging.

I couldn't simply call Blake. He wasn't likely to admit to some stranger over the phone whatever motive he might have had. As cloak-and-dagger as it sounded, I needed to spy on him to see if he'd recently made any large purchases that he might be having trouble paying off or if he showed any obvious signs of money troubles. Those, coupled with the theory of him killing his grandfather because he needed the inheritance immediately, should be enough to redirect the investigators' attention off of me.

Besides, I knew I hadn't killed Harold and almost killed Janie. Whoever *had* deserved to be caught and punished for what they'd done.

My new problem was how to follow Blake around. I didn't have his address. It wasn't like he was going to give me his address if I asked him. The only farce I could think of was to tell him I had a package for him, but no one in Blake's generation would fall for that. Everyone my age and younger had grown up wary of phone scammers.

I already knew he didn't have an open social media profile or a website. But maybe he was still listed.

I opened the browser on my phone, went to 411, and typed his phone number in. A B&D Cartwright popped up, including their address.

THE NEXT MORNING, I GOT UP AT FIVE O'CLOCK AND DROVE TO Blake Cartwright's house. I went past and parked on a nearby cross-street in his neighborhood. It put me close enough to be able to see if anyone left the house.

Thankfully, they didn't seem to have a garage. A garage would have ruined my whole plan. I might have ended up accidentally following D Cartwright around rather than Blake Cartwright.

As it was, I'd likely only have today to try to come up with a solid motive. Not only couldn't I afford to take multiple days off, but my giant purple-and-pink truck wasn't exactly stealthy. After a couple of hours, he'd be sure to figure out I was following him.

After two hours surveilling, I'd decided that cop shows on TV were all lies. Every time they showed anyone on a stakeout, they were always drinking coffee for about a minute before the suspect showed themselves.

Not only could I not drink coffee for fear of needing to use the restroom, but sitting in my truck, staring at the Cartwright house, made me increasingly aware of my isolation. It was no wonder stakeouts were always done with partners. Staying awake and focused would have been a lot easier with someone to talk to.

At seven-thirty exactly, someone finally came out of the house, but it wasn't Blake. It was a petite brunette with a baby in her arms and two children who looked barely school age following behind her.

A dull ache hit me behind the eyes. That was great. I was trying to send a dad of three little kids to prison to save myself. Logic told me that if he was the one who poisoned Harold, he'd brought this on himself, but my heart wasn't convinced.

The woman strapped all three kids in and headed off in the tan SUV from the funeral. It'd looked anything but new. The car that remained in the driveway wasn't any better. Neither vehicle was even an expensive model, and they both looked old enough that car payments shouldn't have been an issue.

I had the unsettling feeling that I'd sent myself on a fool's errand.

I'd almost convinced myself to give up and head to my regular lunch spot early when Blake came out of the house dressed in a suit and tie, looking about as un-criminal as a person could.

But he had been running from the scene of the crime, I reminded myself, and his wife and kids weren't at a birthday party they should have been at.

It'd be hours before my regulars were looking for me. I might as well at least follow him to work and see if a bookie or some equally shady character waited for him in the parking lot.

Not that either of those types of people were likely to be waiting for him at his place of work at this time of the day. Maybe it was a good thing I didn't have a partner on this. That last thought had been me trying to justify the wasted time and gas, and I'd have probably said it out loud if anyone were around to listen to me. They'd have had a great excuse to mock me.

If I spent much more time alone, I might start regularly talking to myself, and that couldn't be healthy. Living in a food truck meant I couldn't even get a pet and legitimize talking to myself by talking to them instead.

Blake pulled out of his driveway, and I followed him from as far back as I felt I could without losing him. Which wasn't far. His car wasn't distinctive enough for me to trust that I could pick it out if a lot of vehicles got in between us.

Instead of going toward the business sector the way his suit suggested he would, he turned west. While there were a few shops that way, none of them were the type where employees wore suits as far as I could remember. None of the restaurants were even fancy enough to have a maître d.

He signaled and turned into the parking lot for Friends Bar.

Not the kind of place I'd expect anyone to go before work in the morning.

Maybe I'd made the right choice to follow him after all. This could point to him being an alcoholic, which could cause all kinds of financial problems. He could also be meeting someone here that he felt he couldn't meet at his home or place of employment. While I'd laughed at myself for thinking he might be meeting a bookie at his place of business, I could see him meeting with someone he owed a large sum of money at Friends.

I pulled past the entrance into Friends' parking lot to give Blake time to park and exit his car without making it obvious I was following him. I turned around in the steakhouse parking lot next door, and then parked in the Friends lot on the far side.

Other than his car and mine, there were only two others in the lot.

I'd been down this way a couple of times, scouting locations where I might park for good weekend foot traffic, and the name of this particular bar had stuck with me. I wasn't sure whether they were playing off the TV show of the same name or if they were alluding to how Cheers had been the bar where everyone knows you and your friends.

Probably neither, if I was being honest, but I couldn't help myself. I liked to try to find connections and reasons for everything. It helped me to feel like life had a purpose and a plan to it and wasn't simply random.

One thing I was sure of—none of the restaurants on this particular street opened before eleven, including Friends.

And yet Blake had gone inside. Someone had been expecting him at 8:30 on a Monday morning when most people were at work or heading there.

The front windows of Friends were mostly glass. If I could get a picture of whoever Blake was meeting, I'd have more to pass over to the police. Anonymously, of course.

If the police could identify the other person as someone who regularly loaned large sums of money, that would scream motive. I'd be free to leave Lakeshore without looking like I was fleeing a crime.

I climbed down from my truck and skirted the edge of the parking lot. If Blake and whoever he was meeting were in eyesight of the window, I didn't want to give myself away. I could probably outrun anyone who tried to chase me, but my truck was so identifiable it wouldn't be worth it.

I tiptoed across the cement and over the lines of grass growing in the cracks. It wasn't like the people inside would be able to hear me coming, but it made me feel better. I stopped at the edge of Friends' large window.

If my legs were double-jointed, I would have kicked myself. The glass was one-way. My ignorance showed how few bars I'd been in in my life. Of course it would be one-way. They wanted to make it feel open, but their patrons wouldn't have loved everyone in the outside world seeing what was happening inside.

That didn't leave me with many options. I guess I could knock on the door and pretend to ask for directions. It wouldn't get me a picture of who Blake was meeting, but I'd be able to give a description. That had to be better than nothing.

Unfortunately, that would mean whoever it was would see me as well.

I hesitated at the edge of the window, rocking back and forth slightly. Fear, for once, kept his opinion to himself, probably because there was no Fear-approved solution here. Any path I took left me in danger. Fear was probably curled into a ball in the center of my mind right now, silently screaming.

Having someone see me seemed like the lesser bad option. They wouldn't know I was the one who gave their description to the police. Even if they figured it out, I should be long gone by then.

The key was for me to look calm and non-suspicious. I'd stopped here in the hope of someone being inside who could give me directions. If I hadn't found anyone here, I would have gone on to the next business until I got the help I needed.

I adopted the walk I used to use when I was out with Jarrod. It said both *Don't notice me* and *Nothing's wrong here.* A stride that wasn't hurried and yet wasn't lagging, without too much hip swing or bounce to my step. Practiced casual.

Two strides from the door, it swung open and Blake came out.

He stopped and let the door swing shut behind him. He gave me the awkward half-smile people get when they're surprised to find someone where they didn't expect them to be. Up close, I could see that his suit was a little too short on the sleeves, as if he'd owed it since before his last growth spurt.

"You're the cupcake lady, aren't you?" he asked. "The one I bumped into in the parking lot at Grandpa's birthday."

He said it so casually, like there was nothing for him to be ashamed of about the last time we'd met other than that he'd knocked me over. Not for the first time, I wished I was a better judge of character. I didn't know if a guilty person would so easily bring up their escape from the scene or not. Maybe they would in order to see how I'd react and gauge whether I suspected them or not.

He was still looking at me as if he expected me to confirm my identity even though the big truck sitting like a purple mushroom behind us should have given it away. Or maybe he was digging for why I was there, at a bar that wouldn't open for hours.

You already came up with a story, I reminded myself. *Stick to it and you'll be fine.* "That's me. I think I might be lost."

He glanced back at the door behind him, and his shoulders drooped like a balloon with a slow leak. "I thought so, too, but it's the right place. But they've already filled the job, if that's what you're here for."

They'd already filled the…he was here to apply for a job?

Applying for a job in person explained his suit and showing up at a business that would technically be closed. The ad must have told people when they could bring their résumés by.

The memory of his three little kids filing out to their SUV behind his wife brought an ache to my chest. You didn't wear a suit to an interview for a job at a bar unless you were desperate. "How long have you been out of work?"

"Almost six months. My wife was a stay-at-home mom with our kids, but she's looking for a job now, too."

The ache in my chest doubled. After six months, their savings were likely gone, assuming they'd had any in the first place.

He stretched a hand out toward my truck. "I wouldn't have expected you'd need a second job."

He couldn't have known how close to the truth he was hitting with the idea of me needing a second job. If I had a social security number to go along with my fake ID, I might have considered actually getting another job to see me through, but all I had was my real SSN. I couldn't give anyone that.

"It's always difficult when I move to a new town until people get to know me. Food services are so much about word of mouth."

I gave myself a mental shake. The conversation with Blake felt so easy and normal, like we were two old acquaintances, that I'd almost forgotten why I came here in the first place. I hadn't come here for that bar job that we'd both apparently missed out on. I'd followed him here to see if he had a motive for killing his grandfather to get an early inheritance.

I'd found a huge, blinking motive. Not for the first time today, I wished I hadn't bumped into Blake in the parking lot and didn't need to suspect him.

My throat closed up, as if the words knew I didn't really want to speak them. "Will your inheritance from your grandpa help out some?"

His eyebrows came together, forming three little vertical lines between them. "My inheritance? Oh right." His eyebrows leveled out, and the corners of his lips turned down instead. "There wasn't anything left to inherit."

I was a good judge of emotions, but I didn't have the natural ability that some people did to tell if they were being lied to. In this case, Blake might have been lying to me, but the way his posture continued to droop suggested true regret to me.

I had to be sure, though. If there was no inheritance, there was no motive for Blake...or for anyone else, as far as I could tell. Without a motive for Harold's death, I might have to start considering a new exit plan—one that left Isabel Addington and How Sweet It Is Cupcake Truck behind.

CHAPTER 11

I widened my eyes just enough to hopefully indicate surprise and not enough to look crazed. "Nothing?"

Blake shook his head. "I guess that's what happens when you have six kids eating up all your money when you're young and then you live to be a hundred. My cousin Claire's been paying for his seniors' home and all his other expenses for close to five years now." Red streaked up his neck. "Not that we all let her do it by herself. I've helped out when I could before... and Dan helps, and I know Stacey was, too, before her mom got sick and needed that operation."

One thing I recognized was when a voice in someone's head was telling them they were a failure, that they'd never be good enough, no matter how hard they tried. Jarrod told me as much so many times that I still heard it in my head every time something didn't go right.

"I'm sure everyone knows you'd like to help more, including Claire."

Her name tasted sour on my tongue. Claire had been paying for Harold's expenses for five years.

Five years where her money was going to cover his needs rather than saving for her own old age, or allowing her to go on vacations, or to buy things she might want. It would be easy for someone to start to resent that. It'd be even easier for someone to fear they wouldn't have enough to support themselves as they got older, especially if they didn't have someone else who would cover for them. Or if they didn't want to put that kind of burden on a family member.

Blake no longer had a motive for killing his grandfather, but it seemed like Claire did.

MY CELL PHONE RANG ON THE DRIVE BACK TO MY REGULAR lunch location. Even though I didn't want to talk to anyone and disrupt my thoughts, I touched the button to answer. I couldn't risk losing a client because I didn't pick up the phone. I answered with my standard greeting.

"This is Detective Labreck, LSPD," a man said from the other end in a businesslike tone. "How are you today?"

My hands jerked, and I swerved across the center line. I pulled my truck back into my lane. The man coming toward me from the opposite direction flipped me the finger as he passed. I couldn't tell exactly what he was yelling at me, but I could guess at some of the names he was likely using.

I tried to tell myself to stay calm and answer normally, but my heart was beating so hard that the words couldn't seem to find a way out around it. It was possible Jarrod had gone through the police to find me. Possible, but unlikely. Another police officer would ask too many questions and might see through any story Jarrod told. This call had to be about Harold Cartwright's murder.

"Good morning, Detective. I'm on my way to my next stop, so I have you on speaker. I apologize for any background noise while I drive."

I used the tone that I used to say *good morning* to Jarrod. Upbeat enough to keep from sounding stressed or tired, but not so chipper that it sounded forced or my listener would wonder what I was so happy about.

"I'll keep this brief, then," the detective said. "I'm overseeing the investigation into Harold Cartwright's murder, and I'm contacting everyone who was there to give a statement."

His voice said *no big deal, all routine.*

I knew better.

I knew enough about law enforcement investigations to know that they weren't going to be talking to me merely as a witness. Everyone who'd been there was both a potential witness and a potential suspect. They'd be watching to see if I was nervous—and I would be, but not because I killed Harold—and to see if my story matched up.

Detective Labreck was still talking, and I forced myself to pay attention.

"We're also asking everyone to give us their fingerprints. We just need to be able to eliminate the fingerprints of people who were supposed to be there. I was hoping you could come down to the station today."

A request, but not a request. I knew that much, too. If I refused, I'd look guiltier.

My hands shook, making it hard for me to control my truck. I pulled off onto the shoulder of the road and put my hazard lights on.

I couldn't give them my fingerprints. I couldn't even give them my full name, and they were sure to want it. Lying to the police about your name and possessing a fake identity were both crimes. Not only would they realize Isabel Addington was a fake name, but they'd be able to match my prints up to my real identity.

The best I could do was stall. "I can't come today. I have scheduled events until late tonight, and then I need to get to bed and be up early tomorrow for another."

"I understand. We all have to work. How about we make an appointment for a time this week that would work?"

Shoot. He hadn't even hesitated. That meant he was expecting me to try to avoid it.

My last hope that I was part of a list evaporated. If I wasn't their sole primary suspect, I was at least one of them. The list couldn't be a long one.

Worse, if I tried to evade a meeting a second time, he'd stop playing nice.

The best I could do was try to buy myself enough time to gather evidence on Claire.

"The soonest I can make it is Friday afternoon. Is there a time then that would work for you?"

Yeesh, I sounded like I was making an appointment for a pedicure or something.

"I'll expect you Friday at two."

That gave me fewer than five days to prove I hadn't killed anyone and to put as much highway between me and Lakeshore as possible.

AS I PARKED MY TRUCK, MY MIND KEPT CHEWING ON WHAT I'D learned from Blake the same way it chewed on a recipe that wasn't turning out quite right.

Claire had seemed genuinely upset at Harold's death, but it was possible she was simply a good actress. That made more sense of her vendetta against me than anything else.

If she'd killed Harold, she'd need to make sure the guilt pointed somewhere else. What better means of doing that than by targeting me? I already had things about me—including being new to town, never giving my last name, and not having a permanent address where I could be found—that made me look shady.

She'd even been smart about not trying to frame me herself. She'd convinced Dan that something wasn't right about me, and she was using him to gather as much evidence as possible to point the finger at me. Dan would be extra-motivated since whoever killed Harold also almost killed his daughter by accident.

I set out the cupcakes. Today's array included tiramisu, even though I'd had it on the menu late last week. One of my regulars had said it was her birthday today, and I knew tiramisu was her favorite.

I took one out of the fridge, added the mascarpone whipped cream on top, and dusted it with cocoa powder. I only put out one of each type for people to see and kept the rest ready to go once someone purchased. Hot weather and whipped cream or hot weather and real buttercream didn't always mix.

I'd been in this spot long enough that some people seemed to be walking down to grab a cupcake and head straight back to work. Even so, the traffic pre-lunch was light enough that I had plenty of time to mull over what to do about my newest discovery.

I obviously couldn't just go to the police with an accusation and no evidence. It'd look like retaliation. Claire wanted them to investigate me, and I wanted them to investigate Claire.

Besides, I needed something solid enough that I could give it to the police and leave with the security that they weren't going to put a BOLO out for me. A hunch that Claire might have killed her grandfather because he was becoming a financial drain and didn't look like he was going to die anytime soon wasn't enough.

I just didn't know where to start. I couldn't follow Claire around the way I had Blake. She'd spot my truck immediately. No one at her bank, or even Harold's seniors' home, was going to talk to me. I wasn't family, let alone Power of Attorney for her or Harold.

A woman I'd seen a few times before stopped at the window and pushed her sunglasses to the top of her head. "Can I have a Cherries Jubilee?"

I had a feeling that running down to grab a cupcake was the only break she took, based on the fact that she always came alone and headed immediately back in the same direction she'd come from. She also didn't pull out her phone while waiting like most people, almost as if her eyes needed the short break from screens.

I assembled the Cherries Jubilee and handed it to her, then pointed to the email address on the chalk board. "If you have any suggestions for making the cupcakes better or for new flavors, make sure to let me know."

She was one of my experimenters—the ones who tried a new

cupcake every time they came rather than defaulting to a trusted few flavors. Those were the best people to get suggestions from. From my experience, they seemed to be on top of the latest trends.

She headed off. Before I could put her cash away, her head bobbed into view again.

She raised up like she was standing on tiptoes to get a better look at me. "Excuse me?"

My heart did a strange double beat, and I concentrated on slowing my breathing before my heart rate ran away with me and made me light-headed. It was probably nothing more than that she'd seen the article and wondered if that was me. Or she'd changed her mind, which wouldn't be great but wouldn't be an end-of-the-world tragedy either.

"It's Isabel, right?" she asked.

I nodded.

She pushed her sunglasses up onto the top of her head again and met my gaze. "Are you okay?"

My vocal cords felt like they were broken. That was the last thing I'd expected. It'd been so long since someone asked me about my well-being that I didn't know whether to laugh it off or be truly concerned that a near-stranger thought to ask. What I would have loved to do was sit down with someone for just a minute and tell them how not okay I was, but I couldn't do that. Not now. Probably not ever again.

"What makes you ask?"

She lifted up on her toes again and set the cupcake on the counter. "I can't be sure, but I think that's barbecue sauce, not cherries."

I bent down slightly for a closer look, but I didn't need it. I could smell the difference as soon as I got close.

My face felt tight and hot, like I'd fallen asleep out in direct sunlight for a couple of hours.

I'd been experimenting with a savory breakfast cupcake full of bacon and chives. The "icing" was BBQ sauce. I must have been so distracted that I grabbed it instead of the cherries out of the fridge.

I swooped the offending cupcake out of sight. "I'm so sorry. I'll make you a new one."

The woman waited without tapping her foot, putting her sunglasses back down in a show of impatience, or even pulling out her phone.

When I handed her the cupcake, she opened her mouth and then shut it again as if she were thinking about repeating her question about my welfare.

Instead she quietly accepted the cupcake and held my gaze again. "I'll be back tomorrow. Take care of yourself."

I couldn't tell her I was trying to and seemed to be failing. It felt like there was an awful lot I couldn't tell people, and I was starting to realize how much I missed it. To have someone, anyone, who I could say to "I'm having a bad day today" or "Today was a great day."

They all blurred together into mediocre days because I had no one to share them with. My life had no one to witness it.

I scooped up the barbecue-iced cupcake and brought it over to the trash can, but I couldn't bring myself to throw it out. Weird flavor combination or not, I'd eat it as lunch. I wouldn't have lunch otherwise, and then at least I wouldn't have wasted it.

I unwrapped it and bit down. The combination of the BBQ sauce with the rum-flavored cupcake wasn't that bad, but it would have been better if it'd actually had cherries with it, too.

It was a good thing that my customer hadn't eaten the cupcake for more than one reason. My barbecue sauce still tasted too much like ketchup.

I choked slightly on my bite of cupcake and coughed.

Ketchup. The almond butter that killed Harold Cartwright was in the ketchup. That meant that Claire either had to have brought the ketchup herself—which seemed unlikely since she was angry at the other food truck vendor for not bringing enough ketchup and mustard—or she'd hired someone who worked for the other vendor to do it for her.

It was an angle the police might not have considered. Even if they had, the person working with Claire wasn't about to confess the moment the police came asking questions. I didn't know what leads the police were following for sure. If they were considering Claire, without a clear connection between Claire and the vendor, the police probably assumed Claire did it herself.

If she'd been smart, she'd have kept her fingerprints off most of the bottles of ketchup, thereby providing herself with an appearance of innocence. None of the vendor's employees would have to explain their fingerprints on the bottles. The police would expect the employees to have touched the bottles while purchasing them, packing and unpacking them, and setting them out.

All of that was presently speculation. I still needed more. I'd sound crazy saying one of the vendor's employees maybe possibly knew Claire and could have been hired by her.

If I could point to a specific employee for them to look at, though, it might be enough.

It was a slim hope, but it was also the only one I had. Time was running out for me.

While I served the rest of the post-lunch crowd, I debated with myself over my options.

The best way would have been to get hired by the burger truck. It'd give me some extra cash, and I'd be able to poke around without drawing a lot of attention to myself.

The problems with that approach seemed to outweigh those benefits, though. That would only work if they were hiring, and it would take time—more time than I had.

Plus, I'd have to give them my real SSN. I'd made that mistake once. The first town I'd gone to, I'd gotten desperate and I'd had to take a job.

And Jarrod found me.

I'd barely escaped. Had it not been for the construction

worker who forgot his lunch box at the site and came back for it, I wouldn't have escaped. He'd thought Jarrod was trying to rape me, and he'd run to my rescue, wielding a crowbar.

The look Jarrod gave me as he ran off was the reason I knew he'd never stop hunting me with the intent to kill me this time. The last time, he'd planned to take me back. My second escape, accompanied by the wound to his pride of how it happened, was something he'd never forgive or forget.

I couldn't be sure the job I'd taken was how he found me, but it seemed the only logical path. I wouldn't take that risk again.

Which left me with going to the other vendor and pretending *I* wanted to hire *them*.

I CALLED SERIAL GRILLERS AND FOUND OUT THEIR CURRENT SPOT, explaining I was considering hiring them, but that I wanted to speak to them first. I'd noticed that business names weren't as creative here as in Fair Haven, but it would have been unusual if they had been. Fair Haven was one of a kind. Serial Grillers was one of the few that could have fit right in.

I parked my truck a block away and walked to the coordinates I'd been given. I'd also taken a few steps to disguise myself, letting my hair down out of its ponytail and putting on a pair of sunglasses and a ball cap.

Like most food trucks, the owner was also the operator, so there was a good chance he'd have recognized me as the cupcake lady from Harold Cartwright's party if I showed up looking like myself. Thankfully, the warm sunshine made the glasses and hat believable.

I strolled up to the truck like I was completely relaxed and stopped at the window. Alongside the owner, whose name was Vinny, according to the sign on the side of the vehicle, I spotted two other guys inside. I knew which one was Vinny because he had to be the one Claire spent so much time yelling at. She wouldn't have chosen an employee over the boss.

"What can I get for you?" Vinny asked.

"I'm…" Great. I hadn't thought up a fake name. I couldn't say Isabel. I'd been in the paper after all. He might put it all together. "I'm Amy."

Wow. That was actually worse. It took all my years of holding emotions in to keep from covering my face. Of all the names that I could have used, I'd defaulted to my real name under pressure.

Now I definitely had to make this worth the risk.

"I'm the one who called," I said.

"Right, right." The man's face had heavy jowls, and when he smiled, they lifted up, reminding me of a grinning bulldog. "Let me come out and you can ask me whatever question you need to."

That wouldn't work. I needed to mention Claire's name

around the full number of truck employees to see how they reacted.

I moved for the door. "Actually, could I come inside for a second. I'm OCD about cleanliness, and one of the reasons I wanted to meet was so I could see your truck." I giggled like I expected him to think I was silly. It felt unnatural. "Too many bad experiences with hot dog stands, I guess."

That last part made me sound even more inane than the giggle. Hot dog stands didn't have much to keep clean.

But Vinny didn't let on if he was thinking I was a few grains shy of a full salt shaker.

He popped open the door from the inside and stepped out of the way. "Be my guest, but it's a tight fit in here with four."

It'd be a tight fit to even squeeze past him into the truck.

I looked up at him, and my feet felt like my shoes had melted into the concrete. Intellectually, I knew that not all men were dangerous. Not all men were like Jarrod. Not all men would hurt me.

But there was this part of me that had to fight every time to remember it because I knew that most men were strong enough that they could hurt me if they wanted to.

I'd take this one step at a time because I had to. If I turned back now, I had no way to continue my search for the person who really killed Harold Cartwright.

I forced my feet into action and focused on details rather than my fear. Like how Vinny smelled like relish and onions, and how both his employees wore hair nets even though one was bald, and how shiny all his equipment was.

If I'd actually been there to inspect the cleanliness, I would have been impressed. No wonder Claire had chosen them. This part of the operation, at least, would have easily met her exacting standards.

But I wasn't here to inspect cleanliness, and this was my best chance to catch his employees off guard.

I shot a smile back over my shoulder at Vinny and then turned so I could watch his employees' reactions. "I'm actually here because Claire Cartwright recommended you."

The bald employee furthest away from me snorted—and not a little snort, either. The man closest to me, who should have been wearing a hair net on his mustache as well given the length of it, cast me a look that said he must be in a Bush's Baked Beans commercial because he'd just seen pigs fly.

Vinny pushed past me, bumping my shoulder. The action was likely accidental given the tight space, but I had to swallow hard to keep from ruining the cleanliness of his truck by throwing up all over him. Fear was screaming so loud in my head for me to get out that I could barely focus.

Vinny grabbed a bottle of ketchup and a jar of relish from a shelf and slammed them down next to the nearly empty ones on the counter. "If you're a friend of Claire Cartwright's, I'm gonna have to ask for full payment up front instead of a deposit. I still haven't been paid."

Maybe Claire wasn't paying him or me because she couldn't. The financial trouble caring for Harold put her in might be more serious than even I imagined. Perhaps she threw his party despite not being able to afford it because she needed a place to poison him that would be full of potential suspects.

Vinny swiped up the old containers and heaved them into the garbage. The ketchup was the same cheap generic brand of the extra bottle at the birthday party, not the specialty brand of all the other bottles.

I'd thought the difference at the party was because of Claire's insistence that they hadn't provided enough. At the time, it'd seemed logical that Vinny sent one of his guys to the nearest store to buy the first ketchup they could lay their hands on and return fast.

Now it looked like it was the other way around. The generic brand ketchup was what they normally used.

If that were the case, though, they shouldn't have had the other ketchup there at all. Even small businesses often made a deal with a particular company to only carry their brand. Not always, but often.

I picked up the new ketchup bottle and pretended to examine the label on the back. "Is this the ketchup you always use?"

Fear tried to tell me that my voice squeaked and that I'd given myself away, but this was one of the times I knew he was a liar. I'd perfected the art of keeping my voice casual when asking questions. It'd helped me avoid angering Jarrod by seeming to question his intelligence or actions. If I kept my voice casual, he took it as curiosity or that I wasn't smart enough to get it.

Vinny's jowls jiggled, and he grabbed the bottle back from my unprepared hand. "What is it with you people and the ketchup? I'll tell you what I told Claire Cartwright. Ketchup is ketchup, and I can't get no different ketchup. It's this ketchup or you can get your own like she did."

Vinny's raised voice sent spikes of numbness shooting through my limbs at the same time as my mind tangled up on the notion that Claire provided the specialty ketchup for the party herself.

Vinny took a step toward me in the small space, and I instinctively backed up and rammed into the drawers behind me. Pain shot through my spine, and I bit back a whimper.

Vinny pushed past me and opened the door up again. "I appreciate you thinking of us for your event, but I don't think we're gonna be the right truck for you. Best of luck."

There was enough sarcasm dripping off his words to make the floor slick. One thing I could say for Claire, she knew how to leave a lasting impression on people.

I stumbled out the door and down the steps.

Claire purchasing the ketchup herself made the most sense if she wanted to easily be able to mix the almond butter in beforehand, but it wasn't very smart. If the police questioned Vinny and his guys about the ketchup, they'd find out that they hadn't provided it, pointing directly at Claire.

And she'd seemed genuinely annoyed at Vinny's crew at the number of ketchup bottles. She was so picky about details that surely she wouldn't have bought the wrong number of bottles and then forgotten she'd provided them so that she yelled at Vinny, causing a scene.

Unless that was her intent. Yell at Vinny so that people heard her, giving her plausible deniability later when Vinny claimed she'd been the one to provide the special ketchup?

Maybe this was enough to take to the police, but surely they knew all this already from talking to Vinny, and they were still looking at me.

I walked away from Vinny's truck, but stuttered to a stop after only two steps.

Dan Holmes stood at the edge of the sidewalk, arms crossed over his chest, his gaze hard enough to leave bruises.

CHAPTER 12

I wasn't afraid Dan Holmes would hurt me. There'd been something in the way he interacted with Janie and with Claire that told me he had too deep a respect for women to ever do the kind of things Jarrod had done.

At least, I wasn't afraid he'd hurt me physically. But physical abuse wasn't the only way a person could be hurt. My career and my freedom were definitely in jeopardy.

I'd already been caught off guard and reacted to his presence, so I couldn't walk by as if I hadn't seen him or didn't know him. Instead, I held my ground and waited for him to make the first move.

He could have been a statue with how still he stayed. "What are you doing here?"

Grudgingly, I had to admire his bluntness. He didn't try to

find out in some roundabout way or even couch it as *Would you like to tell me what you're doing here?*

Though he probably knew that, if he phrased it that last way, I'd have said *No*.

"I was here to talk to Vinny. Food truck operators will often coordinate on events."

The words were out of my mouth before I realized how incriminating that might sound. If Claire claimed Vinny provided the ketchup, and they thought I was the one who tampered with it, my words might make it sound like a conspiracy. We conspired to both get hired and work together to kill Harold.

"Don't listen to that crazy lady," Vinny shouted. "She's not got any part in my business. I wouldn't work with her."

I spun around. He was leaning out the front window of his truck, across his counter. A woman stood in front of the counter, her hand extended in mid-air, a five-dollar bill dangling from her fingers as if she'd been in the middle of paying when Vinny overhead my explanation and decided to set the record straight.

"She came here saying she was looking to hire me," Vinny said, his raised voice easily carrying to where we stood.

Carrying far enough, in fact, that an elderly couple walking by turned to look.

"Then the ketchup I've been using since I started this truck five years ago wasn't good enough for her." Vinny poked a finger in our direction. "So either you both buy something or you leave. You're scaring away the non-complaining, paying customers, and I got a business to run."

There was a story in the Bible where the ground opened up and swallowed people whole. That didn't seem so bad right about now.

I didn't want to turn back around and face Dan. He'd caught me in a blatant lie. No matter what I said from this point on, he wouldn't believe me. I couldn't blame him. I wouldn't believe someone who'd been caught lying to me, either.

Unfortunately, I couldn't avoid facing him. I pivoted slowly back around.

Dan's arms were still crossed over his chest, but his arm muscles looked less tense, and there was a twitch in the corner of his mouth that I would have thought was a smile had he been anyone else, in any other situation.

His arms lowered to his sides. "He doesn't like you much."

And the best thing I could think to say in response was, "Nope."

Dan took a step closer so that we were a normal speaking distance apart. "I know you didn't come here to actually hire him. If I asked you again what you're doing here, would you tell me?"

What would be the point? "It'll sound so crazy you'll never believe me."

His head tilted to one side as if he were trying to take my

measure and couldn't quite manage it. "How about we give it a try?"

He bought two hot dogs from Vinny, which seemed to calm the man down, then motioned for me to follow him to the picnic table a few hundred feet away.

He handed me one of the hot dogs. I hated to accept it. It had to be meant to bring my guard down in the hope that I'd slip up and admit to something that could identify me as Harold's killer. But I was hungry, and I really couldn't afford supper if I didn't accept this.

Worse, there was a part of me that wished—hoped—it were an actual peace offering. That part of me was the stupid part that I couldn't risk listening to.

"So?" Dan asked. "The truth this time. Please."

The *please* almost undid me. Because maybe if I told him the truth and he believed me, I'd have an ally in this hunt.

So I did. I told him the whole story starting with how Claire told me there'd be a way for me to display my cupcakes already set up, and that there wasn't, which was why I had to borrow the ketchup. I told him about Blake running into me in the parking lot, and my suspicion afterward. I told him that I hadn't gone to the police with the information out of fear that it'd make me look guilty and like I was trying to be part of the investigation.

Finally, I told him what I learned from Blake about Claire's strained finances thanks to Harold's long life—leaving out, of course, how I got Blake's information and that I'd basically stalked him.

"I came here today," I said in closing, "because I thought Claire might have hired someone from Vinny's truck to spike the ketchup with almond butter ahead of time."

Dan balled up his hot dog wrapper and tossed it in a perfect arc into the trash can ten feet away. He rested his arms on the top of the picnic table. "I'm guessing hot dog man would have been a lot angrier if you'd accused one of his guys of that. But you did ask him about the ketchup. Why?"

Giving him what I found out felt a bit like giving up my last advantage. He'd know everything I knew, and could very well use it to plug the holes in Claire's story and protect her, framing me in a way that I couldn't wiggle out of.

I met his gaze for a minute. He was handsome, I'd give him that, but handsome faces often hid ugly hearts.

He let out a slow sigh and flattened his hands out on the table. "Look. You don't have any more reason to trust me than I do to trust you. But I loved my grandpa, and I love my daughter. I want to try to find out who really hurt them. If that's not you, you have nothing to fear from me."

That wasn't entirely true. I still had a lot to fear from him. But I didn't believe he would put Janie in danger or let the person who hurt her, however accidentally, go free without punishment.

"The ketchup at the party wasn't supplied by their food

truck. It was a different brand. They say Claire brought it herself."

Dan leaned back and closed his eyes. "That's what they told the police too. Claire says she didn't."

It almost sounded like he believed me. Almost. It was more like when a person believed someone but they didn't want to believe them.

Dan opened his eyes again. He looked over my shoulder toward Serial Grillers, then focused back on me. "Claire thinks you and the owner of the other truck were in it together. That could be a story you both came up with ahead of time, and so you're just telling me what you'd already agreed on. She says the hot dog vendor didn't say anything to her on the day of the party about not bringing the ketchup himself, even when she was yelling at him about there not being enough."

Claire had admitted to yelling at Vinny. That was something I wouldn't have expected about her.

Still, Dan and Claire had a point. Thankfully, it was one I might be able to explain away. Vinny and I did have one thing in common.

"I was afraid that day that Claire would refuse to pay me over the smallest infraction. Vinny might have been afraid the same way. He probably thought it would be better to take credit for finding the special ketchup Claire requested and to have her mad at him for not getting enough than to risk her refusing to pay him because he pointed out she'd brought the ketchup and it was her fault if there wasn't enough. He might have even thought she'd dock his fee because she supplied the ketchup herself. We often run on a small margin."

Dan pushed to his feet. "Wait here, okay?"

He moved far enough away to be out of earshot and pulled out his cell phone. He could be calling Claire, double-checking her story.

Or he could be calling the police.

Run while you have the chance, Fear said. *You'll have a head start.*

I'd be able to duck down a few side streets and maybe reach my truck. But if I did that, I'd guarantee that I lost whatever small seed of trust I might have gained. I'd be guilty in Dan Holmes' eyes.

I knew very little about him, but I had the sense that if I ran now, he'd hunt me down with the same determination as Jarrod, albeit for different reasons. It was hard enough watching out for one person. I couldn't live my life trying to dodge two.

Besides, the information I'd uncovered about Claire seemed to be information the police already had. I had no way to dig into it further. Dan did. He had access to Claire's life. If he turned his attention from me to Claire, he might find something that would also convince the police I wasn't a suspect.

Dan slid his phone back into his pocket. "Blake confirmed your story." The corner of his mouth actually came up in a real half-smile this time. "Looking to get out of the cupcake business and into bartending, I hear."

I cringed. "I didn't tell him that. He assumed."

Dan chuckled. It died too quickly, along with his smile, and I found myself wishing he'd laugh again. There was something warm and soothing about the way he laughed.

"Claire wouldn't have done this," he said. "Her finances are rough, especially with the divorce a few months ago, but she loved Grandpa, too. She took him to every appointment, bought him everything he needed, and she spent months planning this birthday party for him."

He brought his cell phone out again and swiped his finger across the screen. He turned the phone around to face me. Two grinning faces filled the screen. One was Janie. The other was Claire with the sloppiest makeup job I'd ever seen. She had dark blue eye shadow that surrounded her eyes like a raccoon, and her lipstick looked like it belonged on a clown. She even had a smudge of red on her teeth.

"That's from the day Claire let Janie do her make-up," Dan said. "She knew about Janie's nut allergy. Even if she might have gotten desperate enough to hurt Grandpa, she never would have done anything to endanger Janie. The police said there was nut butter in every bottle, and I watched Claire put ketchup on Janie's burger herself."

He jammed the phone back into his jacket pocket. "Claire didn't do this."

I shook my head and shrugged. I didn't know Claire well enough to have his confidence, but I did know one thing. "I didn't do this either."

"Then maybe instead of working against each other, we should work together to figure out who did."

CHAPTER 13

I wasn't a team player. I'd never even been on a team. And life had taught me that it was rare to be able to count on someone else to look out for you. The safest thing was to look out for yourself.

Dan looked like the kind of guy who'd always been a part of a team—a sports team or a work team. Given that he'd been the one Claire called for when Harold collapsed, he was probably a paramedic or a fireman. Teamwork was probably ingrained in his DNA.

I couldn't explain to a man like that why I preferred to work alone. Even if I knew the right words to use, I wasn't about to share something so personal with a stranger.

Which left me trapped. If I turned him down, I'd lose his good will and he might go back to thinking I was behind Harold's murder.

Besides, without his help, I had nowhere to go from here with the information I'd found.

Dan held his hand out toward me. "Partners?"

I nodded, rose to my feet, and extended my hand to him.

His palm was big enough that my hand disappeared inside his. His grip was firm but not alarmingly so, suggesting someone had taught him the value of a good handshake when he was young, but also gave him the self-confidence to use it. The two didn't always go together.

He let go of my hand and took out his keys. "Our first step needs to be to talk to Claire."

Yeah, *that* sounded like a good idea. I wasn't nearly as convinced as he was that Claire couldn't have done this—though that picture of her with Janie did make me question my original theory—and going would tip our hand. She'd know we were checking up on her. "Claire's not going to want me on her property, let alone be willing to discuss this with me."

The edges of his eyes crinkled like he was smiling inside, but didn't want to seem cocky by smiling on the outside. "Leave it to me. I'll drive us there. Then she won't be able to turn you away without turning me away. And she won't turn me away. She's like my second mom even though she's my cousin."

Dan had a rare way with words. Even when I didn't want to believe him, I wanted to believe him. He reminded me a bit of a non-smarmy lawyer in that sense. Unfortunately, it was also a quality that Jarrod had, and that made me disinclined to climb into a car with him.

Even more unfortunately, his argument for driving there with him made enough sense that I'd be silly not to go along with it.

He did seem to be overlooking one important thing, though. "Shouldn't we first ask Vinny if he saw Claire bring the ketchup or if he assumed she did because he hadn't? It seems like his answer should influence what we do next."

The look he gave me said that wasn't a question he would have expected a cupcake designer to come up with. And that he was a little impressed I had.

"He's not going to want to talk to you again," he said.

I sucked in the edge of my lip. I wasn't sure if he was teasing me or trying to keep me away so he could ask Vinny but then lie to me about what he said to protect Claire. The way his eyes crinkled at the edges made me think teasing. And I'd already decided that I didn't believe he would protect someone who hurt Janie, accidentally or not.

It was going to be even harder to work with someone else than I thought. It required trusting them even in little steps like this.

"He probably wouldn't sell me a hot dog or a burger directly even if I offered him double," I said to cover up my hesitation.

"I think he'd take double." There was a smile in Dan's voice.

"Why don't you let me do the talking. You can still stay nearby to hear what he says if you'd like."

I had the feeling he knew exactly what I'd been thinking.

I stayed around the corner of the food truck, within hearing range, while Dan went to the back of the line and waited his turn. Given Vinny's anger at us for disturbing his paying customers, we decided it was better Dan didn't try to cut the line.

Two more people got into line after him, meaning Vinny wouldn't have much patience. He might refuse to answer Dan's question at all.

I leaned around the edge of the truck just enough for Dan to see me. He must have noticed the motion in his peripheral vision because he looked in my direction.

I pointed to the finger where my wedding ring used to be—I still had it in a plastic baggie in a drawer in my truck—and then mimed eating.

Dan's eyebrows dipped a fraction. I repeated the process, and he gave me a slight nod.

"I'd like an order of onion rings," he told Vinny. "And I wanted to ask you a quick question."

The suspicion in Vinny's voice as he agreed was so thick he could have used it as a sauce. But at least he agreed.

"I was just wondering if you saw Claire Cartwright bring that specialty ketchup that she seemed to think was so important?"

The way Dan phrased it was smart. It made it sound like he

was agreeing with Vinny that it'd been silly and unreasonable for Claire to ask for a specific ketchup rather than using the standard one.

"I didn't see her. Did any of yous?"

He had to be addressing his employees. I wished I could see Vinny's face. I had to even trust Dan to interpret it and the employees' reactions. It made my skin itch.

"Nah," one of them said. "They showed up on the table while we were setting up."

Dan must have looked at the other employee or something because he said "me neither" in a tone that made me think he was shrugging along with it.

In less than a minute, Dan came around the corner toward me, an order of onion rings in his hand.

He held it out toward me. "We might need to work on your charades skills. For a second, I thought you were proposing without us ever having been on a date."

I laughed and snagged a few rings, but the laugh felt like it didn't reach all the way inside. Because some day I might wish I could date, and I wouldn't be able to. I'd left Jarrod, but I couldn't divorce him without giving away where I was. Maybe it was old-fashioned of me, but it didn't feel right to date anyone while I was still married. In my mind, I'd be committing adultery.

Thankfully, that wasn't a dilemma I needed to deal with at present. It might never be an issue. I hadn't had much time for dating while I was caring for my dad, and Jarrod was the first man I'd dated after he died. We'd married within six months.

Dan wiped his fingers on one of the napkins he'd snagged along with the onion rings. "Does that set your mind at ease about Claire?"

It did. Judging Claire guilty based on the fact that she'd requested that specific ketchup was circumstantial at best. No one deserved to go to prison for that, and I wanted to see the right person caught almost as much as Dan did. Not only to protect my own skin, but because I couldn't close my eyes at night without seeing Janie's sweet, panicked little face as she struggled to breathe.

But if Claire hadn't put the ketchup there, it did tell us one thing that should help narrow our suspects down. "It had to be someone who knew Claire was going to ask for the ketchup, but also someone who didn't know she wasn't able to get it."

CHAPTER 14

I felt like I was holding my breath for most of the drive from Serial Grillers to Claire's house in Dan's car. I spent the whole time trying to decide if I was struggling to breathe because I accepted a ride from a man I barely knew or if I was struggling to breathe because the thought of facing Claire again spiked a level of anxiety in me that people usually reserved for a root canal. If I kept this up, I'd be on high blood pressure medication before I hit forty.

Claire wasn't out front in her garden this time when we pulled up, but her car was in the driveway, and a silver SUV was pulling out. Silver seemed to be the popular color of the year. I'd seen an increase in cars that shade on the road.

Dan's arms tensed, making his muscles pop out, and a shiver went down my back.

"Claire's ex," he said. "Soon-to-be ex, technically."

The car rolled slowly by us. The man in the driver's seat waved at Dan on the way past. Dan didn't wave back.

"You don't seem to like him much." I almost expected him to say *No kidding, Captain Obvious* in response, but I had to say something. The tension filling the car was so heavy it made my ribs ache.

"I'd rather have dinner with a drug dealer." He glanced into his rearview mirror as if he wanted to make sure the guy was gone. "He left Claire for a woman our age, but he's refusing to actually divorce her because he doesn't want to pay alimony. Claire's lawyer says they'll get the divorce eventually, but Claire didn't need the stress."

I almost asked if he was sure Claire hadn't killed Harold, but I swallowed the words back down. I either had to commit fully to this partnership or not at all. "What was he doing here, then?"

"Probably picking up more boxes of his stuff. He's taking a couple at a time. I think it's to torture Claire."

On second thought, maybe it was a good thing I couldn't date or marry again for fear of Jarrod finding me if I tried to divorce him. I'd picked Jarrod my first time around. There was no guarantee my judgment had improved over the years. I could end up with another Jarrod, or someone like Claire's husband. Not that Claire seemed like the easiest person in the world to live with.

My mom had died when I was too young to remember what she was like or what my parents' marriage was like. My dad told me happy stories, though, so I had to believe not all marriages were bad.

I swiveled around in my seat, but the silver SUV was gone. "Maybe this isn't the best time for me to drop in on Claire."

"Probably not." Dan turned the car off. "But the police have been pushing her, thinking the same as you have about her. It'll be one less thing for her to worry about if we can figure out who killed my grandpa."

From the sound of it, the police had it narrowed down to Claire and me. Those weren't great odds for either of us.

We got out of the car, and I trailed him to the front door. I stayed one step behind him while he knocked.

Claire threw the door open. "What?" A pause. "Sorry, Dan. I thought you were Mike coming back. He was just here."

"We saw him on our way in."

"We? Is Janie sick? She should be at school."

If I hadn't been convinced by what Dan said before, I was by the concern in Claire's voice. A woman who reacted that way over a potential sniffle wasn't someone who'd do anything to risk Janie's life.

Claire stepped out of the doorway and leaned around Dan, likely expecting to find a sick little girl.

Instead she found me.

Her eyes were red as if she'd been holding in tears the whole time her ex was in the house. Her gaze landed on me, and she jumped back as if she'd almost stepped on a snake. The look she turned on Dan was that of a parent who'd just discovered their child had been stealing from them.

"I need you to trust me and listen," Dan said.

I expected Claire to flare up at him the way she had at me and at Vinny. I expected her to slam the door in our faces.

Instead, she stepped back and motioned for us to come inside.

I hesitated for a second before following Dan in. What kind of a longstanding relationship must it take to have that kind of confidence in someone? She hated me. She thought I killed her grandfather. And yet, she let me into her home because Dan asked her to. The only person I'd ever had that sort of faith in was my dad. I'd thought maybe relationships like that didn't exist elsewhere and that I'd never feel that safe again.

Maybe I'd been wrong. Maybe if Jarrod ever stopped hunting me I could one day have a friendship like that. But first I'd have to find someone who I could trust that way again. Those types of people probably didn't come along every day.

That thought sent a tiny sliver of pain sticking into my heart.

Dan continued to lead the way through the house. Brown packing boxes were stacked everywhere. Not only did it seem like Claire had packed up her soon-to-be ex-husband's stuff, but it looked like she was planning to move as well, either for financial reasons or because she couldn't stand to walk through a house where everything would remind her of her ex.

Dan took a seat on a beige leather couch and patted the other side. I assumed that invitation was meant for me. Claire took a chair to his left. The look she gave me made me think she'd scrub the spot where I was sitting after we left to rid it of the taint.

Dan explained to her everything I'd told him, including how I'd pretended to want to hire Vinny the hot dog and hamburger vendor.

Claire's shoulders inched down as he spoke, but the color also seeped from her face, leaving her skin a strange pasty yellow that reminded me of whole wheat bread dough. She'd been sure I'd done this, and now with that theory looking shaky, she had to be afraid of what it meant for her.

She gripped the arms of her chair. "You said the police are sure the crew of the food truck had no connections to Grandpa, and that their bank accounts checked out?"

They clearly had a better relationship with the police than I did to know that Vinny and his crew hadn't received any strange influxes of cash indicating they'd been paid to kill Harold. Of course, I'd been actively trying to avoid the police, so who knew what I'd have discovered if I went in for the interview immediately instead of waiting.

Dan nodded in response to Claire's question. "Isabel thinks it had to be someone else who knew you'd asked for Grandpa's favorite ketchup but didn't know you weren't able to get it. Was there anyone you talked to about it?"

"Angela." Claire's answer was immediate, as if she hadn't had to think about it at all. "But it wasn't her."

Dan turned his head toward me. "Angela and Claire have been best friends since high school."

I couldn't even imagine what a friendship that lasted that long would look like. You'd be more family than friends at that point.

I tried not to envy the fact that Claire had yet another person in her life who she could trust so completely as to not even question her involvement.

"Angela knew I couldn't get Grandpa's ketchup from the food truck," Claire added, with a look at me that said she'd expected me to argue with her statement that it wasn't Angela.

As if she still believed I would blame anyone so long as it took the focus off of me. Really, I couldn't hold that against her. I'd still been questioning her innocence a few minutes ago.

Dan leaned forward. "It wouldn't have been anyone who knew you couldn't get the ketchup. I'm figuring they knew you were going to ask for the ketchup, and so they planned to swap the bottles that were there out with bottles they'd tampered with."

I couldn't help being impressed that Dan had understood what I was getting at with my idea without me having to lay it out.

Claire pressed her fingers in a line above her eyebrows like she was trying to smooth away the tension there. "I can't think of anyone who I would have talked to about those small party details only at the beginning, but not later on."

Whoever came up with the plan to swap out the ketchup had a nearly perfect scheme. The only flaw was they hadn't realized Vinny couldn't get Claire the special ketchup. Had the plan worked as designed, to anyone who asked, it would have seemed like someone from Vinny's truck had to have spiked the ketchup with almond butter because they were the ones who provided it. No one would have realized the bottles were switched.

The trickiest part for the killer would have been swapping the bottles, but they could have done it one bottle at a time, even.

That brought up another idea for how we might figure out who was behind this. "If you have someone at the police station willing to talk to you, maybe you could suggest they check the bottles for fingerprints that appear on all of them. Most people would have only touched a single bottle. The killer would have had to touch them all. They might not have worn gloves. If anyone had spotted them wearing gloves when they placed the ketchup, it would have seemed strange. Who wears gloves in May, right?"

Dan and Claire exchanged a glance I couldn't interpret, but I suddenly felt like I was on the outside, looking in.

Dan rubbed a hand around the back of his neck. "There were only three sets of fingerprints on all three bottles. Claire's from when she took the bottles off your cupcake display, a set they identified as belonging to a woman named Amy Miller, and a set that didn't show up in the system."

No wonder the police were now trying to get my finger-prints. They knew my fingerprints *should* be on all the bottles. They weren't really trying to eliminate the people who were supposed to be at the party from the unknowns. They were trying to make sure my prints matched the third set because then they knew that the person who killed Harold had to be one of the three whose prints were on all the bottles.

It also explained why Dan and Claire were originally convinced I had to be the killer. Because it was either me or Amy Miller.

The problem was, I *was* Amy Miller. The unknown finger-prints belonged to the real killer.

I'd fallen straight into a catch-twenty-two. I couldn't tell them I was Amy Miller. But if I didn't, I'd be sending them on a useless hunt for Amy when the real killer was whoever those other fingerprints belonged to.

CHAPTER 15

You have to say something, Fear prompted me. *You have to lie. They won't protect you.*

I didn't want to lie to their faces. It was one thing to call myself Isabel Addington when it didn't hurt anyone. It was another thing entirely when it could let a killer go free.

But I couldn't get the simple words *I am Amy* to come out of my mouth. "I'm guessing you don't know an Amy Miller. It wasn't someone you invited?"

Claire shook her head.

Dan was watching me in a way that made me want to crawl out of my skin. Like he knew I was holding something back.

I should never have agreed to this. In fact, my desire to stay somewhere—anywhere—had clouded my judgment. I should have tried to run soon enough that I could have sold my truck and bought a new name before the police caught up with me.

Now I had to stay the course and hope we could somehow identify the real killer without giving away my real name.

"The killer might not have planted the ketchup themselves, either. They might have hired someone." I was careful not to say that the killer might have hired Amy. "We still need to think about who would have known you wanted the ketchup but not that you couldn't get it."

Claire rolled her lips together. "There isn't anyone."

Dan rose to his feet. "I have to get going to pick up Janie. Try to think about it some more tonight." He walked over to Claire and gave her a hug. "And don't let Mike keep coming back. Next time he shows up, tell him he needs to take everything he still wants because anything he leaves behind you're going to sell at a yard sale and split the money with him."

Claire nodded and said something in reply, but my brain couldn't catch it. There was one person who Claire might have told about trying to get the ketchup, but who might no longer have been someone she communicated with regularly by the time she learned Vinny couldn't or wouldn't supply it for her.

"Would your husband have had a reason to want to kill your grandpa?"

Claire's hand clamped onto Dan's arm like she needed the support to stay on her feet. "Mike's fingerprints weren't on the ketchup bottles, and I didn't see him at the party."

"When has he ever done anything for himself?" Dan asked.

"You took care of everything. It'd make sense that he'd hire someone to do this rather than doing it himself."

Claire started to shake her head, but then it changed to a nod. "I don't know. There's no reason for him to kill Grandpa except to hurt me. Mike was already leaving me, so it wasn't like he'd have to worry about me spending our money on taking care of Grandpa anymore."

Her voice wobbled, and a muscle twitched in her throat like she was fighting back tears.

Her husband seemed to have no problem hurting her in other ways. Unless his delaying of the divorce and continued presence in her life were for another reason. "Could he have thought that you'd inherit something when Harold—when your grandpa died? I was thinking that could be the real reason he held up the divorce. If you inherited anything while you were still married, he'd have gotten half of it. He could keep coming back, hoping you'd let something slip about it so he can have his lawyer add it to the marital property list."

Claire sank back down into her chair. "Grandpa had a half-million-dollar life insurance policy. It all went to his children, not to us grandkids, but Mike might have assumed that it was left to me because I was the one taking care of Grandpa. He was always asking why I was doing it. He could never understand doing things for someone without an expectation of getting something back in return."

"I'll tell the detective on the case that he might want to check

Mike's financials to see if he paid out a large sum that he can't account for." Dan rested a hand on Claire's shoulder. "If we can't get this resolved soon, though, I want you to come stay with me. His plan might not end at killing Grandpa. If he thinks you got that life insurance money, he might mean to get rid of you, too, once the thirty days have passed."

My hands went cold, and I tucked them between my knees. It all made a little too much sense when Dan put it that way. Some policies only paid out if the beneficiary survived the deceased by a certain number of days.

Claire saw us to the door. She gave my hand a quick squeeze on the way out. It felt like an apology—not only for thinking I was the one who murdered Harold, but also, maybe, for the way she'd treated me at the party. My suspicion was that the real Claire was the woman I'd spoken to on the phone originally. The crazy Claire I encountered later was a woman who was hurt and scared, facing a divorce and a death and financial problems all at the same time.

I hadn't been so far from any of those in my life. I could see how easy it would be to lose patience with the world in general and to want to lash out at someone, even if it wasn't the person who'd caused you the pain.

The clock in Dan's dashboard read 3:15. We'd been at Claire's longer than I realized. Hopefully my truck hadn't gotten a parking ticket. I'd feel honor-bound to pay it.

My stomach growled, and I placed a hand over it. I'd eaten

more today than I normally would, and my stomach seemed to think that was reason enough to start demanding three meals a day again. It couldn't do math. It couldn't understand that wasn't possible. With the summer season coming, things would have gotten better if I didn't need to pick up and move as soon as running wouldn't make me look guilty.

My stomach grumbled again, louder this time.

Dan kept his gaze on the road, which was almost more telling than if he'd looked over. "You mentioned earlier that Claire threatened not to pay you. Did she? Pay you, I mean."

Lying about it would be counterproductive. If he found out I'd lied about being paid, he would doubt everything else I'd said. "No, she didn't."

He drew in a long breath. It made me think he was tired inside though he didn't show it outside. "If you're willing to tag along while I pick up Janie, I'll swing by an ATM and get you what you're owed."

My throat tightened up enough that I couldn't speak, so I nodded instead. Not all men were like Jarrod. Or like Claire's husband.

Some men in the world were still good like my dad. Like my dad and like Dan Holmes.

CHAPTER 16

Janie's preschool was a two-story red brick building attached to a library. The parking lot on the preschool side only had five cars in it when we pulled up. The two still in parallel parking spots across the street suggested that the lot had once been full. It seemed like Dan had been reasonably worried about being late if we stopped by the bank first. Most people had already gone home.

I didn't know if Dan intended for me to wait for them in the car or come inside, but he shut the car off and took the keys. Which made sense. Even though we were working together now, he didn't really know me. I wouldn't have left my car running with a stranger inside, either, just in case they decided they wanted to take it for a joyride.

I followed him from the car. The day had warmed up, and the sun wasn't down yet. Waiting inside a car that wasn't running meant sitting in a pool of sweat. Showers were hard to come by when living in a food truck, and I'd discovered the hard way how messy taking a sponge bath in a tiny sink could be.

Dan hit a buzzer. A woman answered, he gave her his name, and the door clicked, signaling she'd unlocked it.

It'd been years since I was inside a preschool, probably not since I was a kid, but it didn't seem like much had changed. Murals of the alphabet and numbers one to ten covered the walls in bright colors. I peeked in the open doors as we walked by. The rooms didn't have desks like an elementary school would. Instead, tiny chairs in red, yellow, and blue lined low tables.

My baby would have only been a toddler now, but I'd been looking forward to teaching him or her colors and numbers and all the other things they'd need to know before they went to kindergarten.

Dan entered a door on the left.

I hung back and examined the pictures of the teacher and teacher's assistant taped to the door with their names underneath. The kids wouldn't need to find their room on their own, so the pictures and names were probably there to help forgetful parents.

A woman holding the hand of a boy who skipped along beside her passed by and gave me a sidelong glance that clearly said *what are you doing here without a child?*

Slipping into Janie's classroom with Dan seemed better than standing in the hallway, drawing attention to myself. Some parent might think I shouldn't be here and call administration to have me evicted.

I edged into the room. Janie sat on a chair near the corner, her head down and her little arms across her chest. I didn't need a lot of experience with kids to know something wasn't right.

Dan stood on the other side of the desk talking to the teacher's assistant. Her mouth was turned down at the corners. Dan's expression was harder to read than Sanskrit. He seemed even better at hiding his emotions than I was.

I turned my back to give them privacy. I'd only be a part of their lives briefly, and I wouldn't have wanted a stranger over-hearing my personal business even if I'd been living a normal life under my real name.

A banner on the wall I now faced said *Our Favorite Spring Things*. Crayon drawings covered the wall under the banner, and on each, a grown-up had written a short description of the items in the drawings. Which was good, because, in a lot of them, I wouldn't have been able to tell if it was a bird or a flower if there hadn't been a description below.

I searched the wall until I found Janie's. She'd drawn a yellow flower—either that or the sun—a beige rectangle inside a red rectangle, and a tree with a swing. The words next to it said her favorite things about spring were being able to use the swing in her backyard, daffodils, and Great-Grandpa's birthday party barbeque. I wasn't quite sure what a red rectangle had to do with Harold's birthday party, but she must have explained it to whoever labeled the picture. It was probably a hot dog, and she got the colors reversed.

I turned away from the wall. If she had the same project to do next year, she wouldn't be able to choose her great-grandpa's birthday. My chest hurt just thinking about how excited she must have been driving there that day compared to how she must feel now. Whoever killed Harold took what had once been something a little girl looked forward to and broke it.

Dan and Janie headed in my direction. Janie looked at me, stopped, and then sprinted for me. I dropped to one knee, opened my arms, and caught her. She held on so tight it hurt, her body shaking as she cried.

My brain flashed a *does not compute* sign. It could be a reaction to me saving her life. Maybe seeing me again triggered that sense of fear and then relief that she didn't know how to put into words. Or it could be that whatever had upset her at school that merited such a serious conversation made her feel threatened in some way. I'd saved her once, so now she felt like I was a safe haven?

The reason didn't matter. Not to me. I hadn't been able to protect my baby. Jarrod made sure to tell me that it was my fault our baby died. That I'd made him hit me. He'd been right and he'd been wrong. I hadn't made him hit me, but I should have left before he could. I should have left the moment I found out I was pregnant. I should have protected my baby.

Maybe saving Janie made up a little for what I'd done—or rather, hadn't done.

"Sorry," Dan whispered. "It's been a rough day. We're going to have to have a talk about lying and about lying about lying."

Janie said something against my shoulder that sounded like *I didn't lie*, but I couldn't be sure.

A part of me wanted to stick up for her—to make sure that she wasn't being falsely accused. Apparently, I had maternal instincts even though I hadn't mothered a child.

The larger part of me recognized that instincts didn't make me Janie's mother. Dan was her parent, and he had the right to parent her in the way he saw fit. I clamped my lips shut and held her while she cried it out.

When she let go of me, Dan placed a hand on her back and shepherded her out the door. She stomped ahead of him, her bottom lip still sticking out a bit. She dropped back behind Dan and in front of me as we exited the school.

Dan stopped and patted the pocket of his jeans. "I set my keys down on the desk, and I left them there. Wait with the car. I'll be right back."

He returned to the school door and pressed the button again. Janie continued her stomp-walk past the passenger side of Dan's car. Her car seat must be on the driver's side.

I started to sit down on the curb, but stopped halfway and stood up again. Janie hadn't gone around to the other side of the car. She'd continued on toward the road.

She looked both ways, then stepped out into the street.

My heart beat kicked up, feeling like it was beating in my throat rather than in my chest. All I could think was that Dan must normally park across the street when he picked her up, and she was obeying his command to wait with the car. There was a black car that looked almost identical to his in one of the parallel parking spots across the street.

Thankfully, she'd carefully looked both ways so she shouldn't be in danger of any cars, but I still needed to catch her. She was already in the middle of the street. I didn't want her coming back alone.

I strode after her.

A car wheeled out from the library side of the parking lot, accelerating as if it didn't see her.

I yelled her name. She stopped and looked back at me, which only made it worse. She was standing directly in the path of the car.

CHAPTER 17

The driver had to be on their phone not to notice her. I ran for her. I should have watched her better. I was the grown-up. Dan left her with me, trusted her with me for a few minutes.

The car kept coming. I sprinted the last few steps, grabbed her up, and leaped, trying to twist in the air so I didn't fall on top of her.

My shoulder slammed into the ground, and my head bumped the cement. Pain seared through my upper body, making me feel like I was on fire.

For a second there was an avalanche of sound—tires squealing, Janie crying, a man's voice calling our names.

It had to be Dan's voice calling our names.

The pain felt like it was crushing me, but I knew pain. If Fear and I were frenemies, then Pain and I were archrivals. I concentrated on my breathing and turned my mind away, imagining that I was building a wall brick by brick that pain couldn't get through.

I rolled into a sitting position, bringing Janie with me.

Dan dropped to his knees by our side. He reached for Janie, and she crawled into his arms. "Are you okay? Does it hurt anywhere?"

She shook her head against his chest. "I looked both ways, I promise."

"I think she thought this was your car." The words were hard to find. I patted the tire of the car behind me. "The car seemed like it didn't see her."

The driver could have stopped to see if we were alright afterward, but they were probably afraid they'd be charged with something by the police if they did. That's what I would have been afraid of. Since they hadn't actually hit us, there'd be no damage to their car, and they'd be almost impossible to find if they sped off instead. That'd be a tempting option for a lot of people, especially if the driver was on their phone the way I suspected.

"Did you get the license plate?" Dan asked.

I shook my head, but the motion sent Pain breaking through my mental brick wall. My vision tilted like someone had put the world in a snow globe and was shaking it.

Dan held Janie close with one arm and fished around in his

pocket with his other. "I'm calling 911. We need to make a report and have you checked out at a hospital."

"I'm fine." Now who was the liar? "I don't need a hospital." And I certainly didn't want the police taking down my name in a report. "I'd rather just go back to my truck."

"You're not fine. You're bleeding." He touched the back of his own head.

I put a hand to my scalp where I'd hit the cement. The touch of my fingers stung, and my palm came away red. "Head wounds always bleed a lot. I just need to put some pressure on it."

Dan gave me a look like I'd grown a third eye and a tentacle.

You said too much, Fear said. *Pain is making you weak.*

It was probably a sign of how lonely I'd been—how lonely I was—that I personified my emotions.

"If it's about the money," Dan said, "you don't have to worry. I'll cover your medical bill."

Arg. I hadn't even thought about the bill I wouldn't be able to pay if I needed medical attention. That added yet another reason not to go, even though Dan said he'd pay for it.

I struggled to my feet. "I've survived worse. I promise. Get Janie checked out, but I'll be okay. I'll wait in the car."

Dan got up as well, holding on to Janie's hand.

I took a step forward, and the ground moved again. Dan darted forward and wrapped an arm around my waist, holding me up.

His arm felt warm and strong, and for a second, I just wanted to lean on him and let someone else carry the burden—of everything.

"I'll help you to the car and check you over, but then I'm calling 911."

We crossed the street, his arm around my waist and Janie clamped onto his other hand. He helped me into the passenger seat and gently probed my shoulder. The pain in my shoulder had already eased significantly. He had me follow his finger with my eyes, and then even pulled a flashlight out of the glovebox and checked my pupils.

I blinked against the light. "Do you actually know what you're doing with that thing?"

He smiled, but continued his exam. "I was almost a licensed paramedic before I realized that wasn't the career for me."

That explained why Claire called for Dan when Harold collapsed.

He put the flashlight away and pulled a wad of paper napkins from the same glovebox. He handed them to me. "I still think a doctor should see you."

I shook my head. The world stayed in place this time, and I pressed the napkins to my scalp. "I'm feeling a bit better already."

He took his phone back out of his pocket.

I held up a hand. My stomach felt like it was trying to fold into an origami animal. I knew what he'd think when I asked, but I had to ask. "Please don't tell them it was me who saved Janie. You could say *a woman* and that she left afterward. I did leave afterward. It's not a lie. The only useful thing I can say is the car was a light color. I didn't see if the driver was a man, woman, or yeti."

The look Dan gave me made me feel like he was trying to listen in on whatever was going on in my brain.

He didn't say anything in response. Instead, he led Janie back to the side of the road and they sat on the curb. Within minutes, a police car and an ambulance pulled up. The paramedics looked Janie over while Dan talked to the officers. I watched it all in the rearview mirror. Thankfully, he never motioned toward the car.

I lost track of how much time passed before the ambulance and police cruiser left. Dan buckled Janie into her car seat, and she drifted off almost immediately.

"Is she okay?" I asked.

"Clean bill of health." Dan eased his car out of the empty parking lot. He glanced in my direction. "I'm going to give you a choice. I can either take you to the hospital to be looked over or you can come to our house for the night."

For the briefest second, I thought he was threatening to expose me unless I slept with him.

"You might have a mild concussion," he said, "which means someone needs to check on you regularly."

I'd been injured in the process of saving his daughter. In his mind, that must have created a debt he now needed to somehow repay.

Thankfully, I hadn't voiced my original thought.

"I'd feel responsible if I let you go home alone and something happened to you," he continued.

Right. He didn't realize I lived in my truck. He'd definitely insist on me staying with them if he knew that.

The lure of a hot shower and a soft bed for my achy body was more than I could stand. Staying with them also ensured one sound night of sleep. Jarrod would have no way to find me since Dan and I were practically strangers.

We pulled up at a stop sign.

He pointed right. "My house. You can sleep in Janie's bed. She'll want to stay in my room tonight anyway with everything that's happened." He pointed left. "Or the hospital."

"Go right."

CHAPTER 18

Dan asked if we needed to swing by my place to pick up clean clothes first. "My place" was parked over by where Vinny's food truck had been, and I couldn't let him know I slept in my cupcake truck. That was probably a health code violation.

I told him I lived on the far side of town, and it'd take us too far out of the way.

Dan and Janie lived in an older subdivision on a street filled with oak and maple trees. Swaying patches of light and shadow covered the whole street. I hadn't been to this part of town before. It was all residential except for the playground within walking distance of their house.

I didn't know the people here, but I felt like I did. I'd grown up in a similar neighborhood, except we had had palm trees. There'd be swing sets in a few of the backyards, pools in others.

In the summer, kids would ride their bikes around the cul-de-sac at the end, and their parents would feel safe letting them do so. Most evenings, you'd smell someone grilling steaks or hamburgers in their backyard.

Dan showed me Janie's room and then gathered up a towel, a fresh bar of soap, and a t-shirt and pair of sweatpants for me. Given the size, they were his. I'd have to roll up the hems of the pants to keep from tripping on them, but at least I wouldn't have to sleep in my dirty clothes.

As I cleaned up, I couldn't help but think about the differences between men and women. As a man, Dan felt safe inviting a near stranger into his home. He'd smartly orchestrated a way to keep Janie with him at night just in case, but he wasn't afraid of me. Had the roles been reversed, I wouldn't have felt safe inviting a man I barely knew into my home. I didn't know any woman who would.

When I came back downstairs, Janie was playing with model horses in front of the living room couch. Clanging noises from the kitchen suggested Dan was making supper.

I should probably have offered to help, but the couch called too loudly to my bruised body.

Janie ran a horse across the top of the coffee table. "Daddy's making food and phone calls."

One would hopefully be to whoever he had a connection with in the police department. The sooner the police started to look into Claire's soon-to-be ex-husband, the better.

She abandoned the horse on the table and scooted to the edge of the couch. "Will you read me a story?"

"Sure."

I might as well enjoy some of the fun parts of having a child around while I could. My dad reading to me was one of my happiest memories. Not only had he read to me, but once I reached high school, we kept going, either taking turns reading chapters or reading the same books and talking about them. When I left Jarrod, I'd also had to leave behind my collection of books. He'd probably burned them all by now out of spite.

She scurried off and came back with two books clutched to her chest. She crawled up on the couch beside me and laid the books out on her own lap. One had a giraffe doing a pirouette on the cover, and the other had a colony of ants. Janie must be an animal lover.

"Which one should we start with?"

She handed me the one with the ants. I read the story through, giving each character its own voice. The plot revolved around one little ant who couldn't keep the secrets that the other ants told him, and it cost him all his friends because no one trusted him.

Since it was a kid's book, it had a happy ending. It was too bad that the problems in life couldn't be fixed as easily as a children's story book.

I closed the board book and handed it back to Janie.

She stared at the cover. "Daddy thinks you're keeping secrets."

Dan wouldn't have told Janie that, so she must have overheard. Rule of thumb number one with kids seemed to be never to say anything within their earshot that you didn't want repeated. Dan probably hadn't even realized Janie was eavesdropping.

The real question for me was one of timeline. "When did he say that?"

"Tonight. On the phone." She frowned down at the book in her lap. "I don't like secrets."

Ouch. Nothing like being reprimanded by a four-year-old. Having a child tell me how wrong I was would have been a part of motherhood I probably wouldn't have enjoyed.

I should have been surprised that Dan still had questions about me given he'd invited me into his home, but I wasn't. Something in his expression when I'd been asking him not to tell anyone that I'd saved Janie had been sitting uncomfortably in the back of my mind. He might have even had an ulterior motive for inviting me here. He might hope to learn what I was holding back.

But he also had respected my request. Whatever he thought I was hiding, I had to believe he wasn't trying to prove I'd killed Harold anymore. No father would invite someone they believed was a murderer into their home with their child. Right?

I picked up the book with the giraffe on it, but I didn't open the cover. I still owed Janie some sort of response. "Not all secrets are bad. Some secrets are good secrets, like if you're throwing someone a surprise party. And sometimes grown-ups have to keep secrets for other reasons, too. Like when telling the truth would put someone else in danger."

It was the closest I could come to telling her I wasn't a bad person just because I was keeping a secret. I couldn't stand the idea that she'd think I was a bad person. The memory of her throwing herself into my arms because she believed I was a good and safe person was one that would keep me going on days when it felt like it was pointless to keep trying to have a better life.

She pulled at her bottom lip with one hand and flipped through the pages of the ant book with the other. "How do you tell a good secret from a bad one?"

"I think a good secret makes you feel good about keeping it, and a bad secret doesn't."

The complicated part as an adult was that some secrets could make you feel both good and bad. I felt good that I'd been able to reinvent myself to stay safe from Jarrod. It'd taken determination I hadn't been sure I had. I felt good that I was brave enough to leave and do what it took to protect myself.

I felt terrible that I had to keep that secret from every person I met. I felt even worse that my secret might jeopardize the hunt for Harold Cartwright's real killer.

But not bad enough to give them my fingerprints and have

them match Amy Miller's. If I did that, there was no way Jarrod wouldn't know exactly where I was.

Dan cleared his throat from the doorway. "Supper's ready."

I couldn't help wondering how long he'd been standing there.

WHILE DAN PUT JANIE TO BED, I ENDED UP ALONE ON THEIR couch, with nothing to occupy myself except trying to remember any more details about the car or the driver.

I'd been so intent on getting Janie out of the car's path that I hadn't bothered to look at the driver. I couldn't have told the police anything about them. I couldn't even be sure if the car was white, tan, or silver.

Now that the shock of it was wearing off, something wasn't sitting right. The fact that they hadn't slowed down at all still bothered me. My first thought had been that they must have been on their phone, but it was a school zone. What kind of person is on their phone in a school zone? On their phone, in a school zone, driving over the speed limit—as far as I could tell.

It was almost like they wanted to run Janie down as she crossed the street.

But that made no more sense than someone wanting to kill a hundred-year-old man.

Dan came back into the living room and leaned on the wall

by the door. There was a tiredness to his stance that I hadn't seen before. During the day, he'd been all confidence and bravado and strength. It was like watching a knight crawl out of his armor at the end of a battle.

"She's asleep," he said. "Thank you again for saving her. Twice."

He didn't say any of the clichés like he didn't know what he'd do if he lost her. Or how important she was to him. He didn't need to. I could see it. He reminded me of how my dad had been with me. We'd talked about it once I was in high school, how much pressure he felt to try to be both a mom and a dad to me.

Which raised the question of where Janie's mom was.

Dan hadn't seemed to call anyone but the police when the car almost ran us down. Maybe he called Janie's mom after we got back to the house, but Janie hadn't mentioned her mom to me, either. And Dan appeared to have full custody.

As hard as it was for me to comprehend, parents in custody battles did strange things. Maybe Janie's mom felt like, if she couldn't have her daughter, Dan shouldn't have her, either. Or maybe she'd planned to swerve at the last minute, scaring Janie but not hurting her, and using the near miss as evidence that Dan wasn't a fit parent.

He pushed away from the wall. "Would you like a cup of coffee?"

I'd never sleep if I had coffee this late. "I'll take hot chocolate if you have it."

A ghost of a smile passed over his lips. "Hot chocolate it is."

He disappeared into the kitchen and came back a few minutes later with two mugs. He handed me mine and took a spot on the opposite end of the couch, angling to face me.

I felt weird broaching the topic of what happened today. I might simply be paranoia, and then I'd be adding extra fear onto him.

I also didn't want to make it sound like I was asking about Janie's mom because I was trying to figure out if he were single or not. That would create a whole barrel of awkward that I didn't need.

The best way seemed to be to make it sound like I was concerned about her mom. "Did you call Janie's mom to tell her what happened?"

"Her mom's dead. Both her parents are. I did call Claire." He pointed toward a bookshelf where a wedding picture sat. The man in it had the same nose and brow-line as Dan, a similar shape to his jaw, but he was huskier and shorter. "My brother and his wife died in a motorcycle accident when Janie was eighteen months old. I adopted her. I guess I could have raised her to call me Uncle Dan, but I'm the only dad she's going to know, and every kid deserves a dad if they can have one."

I didn't know what to say to that, but I gave him a smile from my heart this time.

Then I remembered why I'd asked about her mom in the first place, and the smile died out of my heart. "It seems like too big a coincidence that someone killed your grandfather and now a car almost runs down your daughter."

I let the idea hang in the air. I couldn't bring myself to suggest that maybe someone was actually trying to hurt him. Because saying it would have hurt him, and for whatever reason, it hurt me to think about doing that. His kindness had found a crack in my defenses big enough that the welfare of this family mattered to me when it shouldn't have.

Dan set his cup aside. "It's not impossible that this is about me. If the two are connected, we could be wasting our time looking at Mike. He's an...a jerk, but he wouldn't have any reason to hurt Janie."

"What about the ketchup, though?"

Dan pressed the heels of his hands against his temples and ran them backward like he was trying to force the tension out of his head. "We might be overthinking it. Claire's gotten that ketchup for Grandpa's birthday party every other year. If someone attended in the past, it'd be easy enough to assume that it'd be the same ketchup this year. Grandpa worked for that company his whole life, and he swore he could tell the difference when someone gave him a different ketchup."

I should ask Dan who would want to hurt him, but it felt too intrusive. He hadn't argued that no one would want to hurt him, which suggested he had a couple ideas of people who might. He just wasn't ready to share them.

Instead of saying anything more, I gulped down the rest of

my hot chocolate. I could tell it came from a package. If I ever got the opportunity, I'd make Dan and Janie real hot chocolate.

The hot chocolate burned my belly. I wouldn't get a chance to do that. As soon as I wasn't a suspect anymore, I'd be gone from Lakeshore. Gone from their lives. And I wouldn't be coming back.

CHAPTER 19

Dan and I talked late into the night, at first tossing around theories about the case but then it moved to his challenges as a single dad and why I loved baking. Part of me worried he might be digging for more information on me, but it felt so good to talk to someone. I even went so far as to give him some tips from my experience as the daughter of a dad doing it on his own.

I didn't die in the night from my injuries, and in the morning, I made Dan and Janie French toast. And realized how spoiled I'd gotten in Fair Haven because of Nicole Fitzhenry-Dawes' pure maple syrup. The imitation maple syrup from the grocery store didn't satisfy in comparison.

Dan dropped Janie off at school, swung by the bank and got me the money Claire owed me, and then brought me to my truck. A yellow slip waved at me from under the windshield wiper.

A parking ticket. Perfect. Exactly what I didn't need.

Dan climbed out of the car with me and plucked the ticket off the truck before I could reach it. "I'll take care of this. It's the least I can do."

He doesn't really want to help you, Fear said. *He just wants to use the ticket to try to get your last name.*

Fear could be right or wrong. Dan probably did still want my last name, but if I didn't at least try to trust someone who'd been kind to me, I'd never be able to trust anyone ever again. I didn't want to be that kind of person. That kind of person lived and died alone.

Besides, he couldn't get my last name from my parking ticket. Even if he managed to get information on my truck, it was owned by a numbered company I'd set up.

So all I said was, "Thank you."

He still didn't move back to his car, like there was something more he wanted to say. He put both his hands into his pockets. It felt like a little boy was suddenly standing in front of me rather than a grown man.

He pulled a folded piece of white paper from his pocket and handed it to me. I slowly unfolded it.

The paper had a black-and-white line drawing of a kitten with a sock on its head and the words *Come Join Us for a Production of Mitten the Kitten and the Very Bad Day*. The date and time were for tomorrow night. He'd actually been telling the truth when he called and said his daughter was in a play.

Dan shifted his weight. "Janie asked me last night if you were going to come to her play. I told her I didn't know but that I'd ask you."

Weight hit my chest like I'd been kicked below my collar bones. He couldn't know what an invitation like that meant to me. To feel like I was wanted and welcome.

There was no way I could go. I couldn't get more attached to that little girl. It'd only be worse for both of us when I had to leave.

And yet I wanted to go more than I'd wanted anything in a very long time—other than to stay alive, of course.

"I'll check, but I don't think I have anything else planned," I said before I could stop myself. I'd give myself that one last happy memory before I left Lakeshore.

If things didn't turn around in the investigation soon, I might have to leave right after the play in order to get as far away as possible before Friday when I was supposed to meet with the detective.

I opened the passenger-side door and tucked the invitation into my glove box, then turned back to Dan. I didn't have a lot of experience with boundaries. Did that invitation mean I could give a suggestion about Janie or not? I wasn't exactly a family friend. I was some weird lady who he originally thought was a murderer and now wasn't quite sure what to think about.

But it'd bother me if I didn't say something. This was probably my last chance.

"Did the teacher's assistant tell you what Janie lied about?"

He shook his head. "She wasn't the one who heard it, but Janie's teacher had an appointment and couldn't wait since I was late."

"Get the full story before you punish her, okay?" Heat was already riding up my cheeks. "It's easy to believe a person in a position of authority just because they're in that position, but they're not always the one you should believe."

A little Edison lightbulb went off in my brain. That's why it'd bothered me. It bothered me because I'd once been the person who was afraid no one would believe her. I hadn't tried to leave Jarrod earlier because he told me everyone would side with him *if* they even believed me.

Something I couldn't interpret flitted across Dan's face. He opened his mouth, and his phone rang. "Just a second."

He pulled the phone out and slid his finger across the screen. "Holmes."

"We got a warrant for her fingerprints." The voice coming from Dan's phone was just barely loud enough for me to hear. "We'll serve it on her tomorrow and hold her until the results come in."

My hands went numb, and I turned away and pretended to examine a scratch on the side of my truck.

"If the fingerprints match, we'll have her name and enough to dig into her financials. Any unusual deposits and we'll have our arrest."

My actions must have tricked Dan into believing that I couldn't hear what was going on because he hadn't moved away.

The police didn't normally share those types of details with civilians, not even with members of the victim's family. Not until after an arrest had actually been made. And Dan seemed to know exactly what *she* the person on the other end of the line meant.

I had a bad feeling I did, too. Detective Labreck hadn't believed that I would show up on Friday and give my fingerprints willingly. He'd decided to take the initiative, rightly figuring I'd stick around for a few days since I thought I had until Friday.

My breath lodged in my throat. I was an idiot. There was only one reason the detective would call Dan with that kind of information. I should have seen it.

His ability to hide his thoughts and emotions. His connection in the police department that gave him more information than anyone would normally have access to. Even his quick willingness to deal with my parking ticket.

Dan was a cop.

And I'd been used.

CHAPTER 20

Dan's invitation to stay at his house last night *for my health* had really been about making sure he knew where I was. His invitation to Janie's play had been about making sure the police could find me to serve their warrant for my fingerprints.

Even his farce of working together had all been to see if I'd slip up. When I didn't offer my fingerprints after we talked about the killer's fingerprints needing to be on all the bottles, that'd probably convinced him of my guilt rather than the other way around.

And he'd only been humoring me when I suggested Harold's death and the car trying to run Janie down might have been about someone trying to hurt him. He'd never believed me. He thought it was me trying to turn the attention elsewhere.

I had to get out of here, out of Lakeshore. Now. Without anyone realizing that's what I planned to do.

I straightened up and turned back to face Dan. I tacked a smile on my face. It'd fooled Jarrod enough times even though we'd been married for years. It should fool someone who didn't truly know me and never would.

"I have to get going," I whispered and motioned toward my truck. "I'll see you guys tomorrow."

I strode around the front of my truck and climbed in as if nothing were wrong. I even waved to him.

That was one thing I could thank Jarrod for. I knew how to act. I knew how to fake a smile and lie to a person's face in the name of self-preservation.

I pulled out onto the road. It didn't look like Dan planned to follow me.

I turned off of the side street onto a larger road that should take me out of town. My windshield was blurry, so I flipped on my windshield wipers. It hadn't looked like rain before. The windshield wipers dragged across my windshield, but the wetness didn't clear.

Something dripped off my chin.

It wasn't raining. I was crying.

I DROVE FOR AN HOUR WITHOUT STOPPING, HEADING IN THE direction of Detroit. That seemed like the best place to disappear. It shouldn't be too hard to find someone willing to sell me a new identity, even if it did strip my bank account bare.

I had a backup set of license plates stored with my spare tire, but I'd have to find somewhere to get the truck repainted in the next twenty-four hours. The BOLO for me and my vehicle would describe it well enough that an officer who spotted me would pull me over and detain me whether the plates matched or not.

I refilled my truck's fuel tank with enough to get us to Detroit, but I pulled my phone out before heading back onto the highway. Even if I reinvented myself again, I had one connection I didn't want to lose.

I have to ditch this phone, I typed to Nicole. *I'll text you when I have a new one.*

A response dinged in almost immediately. *Are you okay?*

The simple answer was *no,* but instead I gave no answer at all. Nicole knew more about my situation than anyone. If I told her I wasn't okay, she'd want to rush in and rescue me. If I told her I was okay, she'd know I was lying, and she'd want to rush in and rescue me. Rescuing people was what she did, especially if she cared about them.

I climbed back into my truck and got back on the road.

My phone rang from the passenger seat. I couldn't reach it to check who it was. Odds were good it was Nicole. Not answering now would only make her panic. That wasn't fair. We weren't close, but she was the closest thing to a friend I had. Maybe I should have waited to text her until I had my new phone. It'd been weakness on my part that I'd felt the need to reach out to someone who hadn't betrayed me.

I hit the button on my display to answer my phone and said a simple *hello* rather than my usual spiel.

"Isabel?" The voice from my speakers was Dan's, not Nicole's.

"Speaking," I said, as if I didn't recognize his voice.

"It's Dan. Holmes." He added his last name like he was worried I would know so many Dans that I wouldn't know which one was calling me. "You left your jacket in my car. I'm heading into work now, but can I meet you somewhere later to return it?"

I glanced at my passenger seat. My jacket wasn't there. That part of his story checked out, and his voice didn't give anything away. But Fear was telling me that it was a trap. He was checking in on me. He suspected that I'd heard his phone call.

Either way, I certainly wasn't going back for it. "I have a full day ahead. Hang on to it for me, okay?"

That should satisfy him since I'd said I would try to make Janie's play. I took the next exit, thankful that I'd looked up the route beforehand rather than relying on my GPS. The last thing I needed now was my GPS telling me which way to go and giving me away.

"I think it'd be better if we got it back to you today so we don't forget where we put it or slop food on it."

His tone seemed light, but there was a forced undercurrent to it.

He was digging. He suspected I was going to run. He might even suspect that I was already running.

"That's okay," I said. "It's an old jacket, so I'm not worried if anything happens to it."

We were back to circling each other the way we had during that early call when he tried to hire me to bake cupcakes for Janie's play in order to get my last name. Last time, he'd given up when I'd run him into this type of a corner.

Silence stretched on his end of the line. The telltale static rumble of someone talking on their speaker in their car told me he was still there. We hadn't lost the call.

He drew in a long breath. "Did you overhear my phone call?"

So we had made some progress in our relationship, if you could call it that when it was built on lies on both sides. We at least knew each other well enough now that he wasn't going to give up when I called his bluff. It showed me a level of respect.

I'd show him the same respect. "I did."

Now the question would be whether he would admit that the person he was talking to wanting to serve a warrant on me. Whether he would admit he was a police officer.

"Isabel." He said my name softly. He had to have guessed by now that it wasn't my name, but it was still the name I'd given him, the name I went by. The only name he knew. "Did you kill my grandfather?"

My foot jerked on the gas pedal, and my truck jumped forward. Of all the things I thought he might say, a blunt question about whether I was a murderer wasn't one of them.

I turned off into a service center. This wasn't a conversation I could concentrate on while also safely driving.

I put my truck into park. I thought about telling him that I wasn't involved in his grandfather's death and confirming that I was only there that day because Claire hired me to provide cupcakes. All of that would have been true. I felt like arguing that my investigation into what had happened and trying to find the real guilty party should have proved my innocence.

But I settled on a simple "No."

He was either going to believe me or he wasn't. That would be his choice. If he didn't believe my *no*, he wouldn't believe all the explanations in the world. And it didn't matter what he believed anyway. It shouldn't matter.

"Have you committed some other crime?"

I rested my head on my steering wheel. That one was so much more complicated. I had, but not the kind he probably meant. I hadn't killed anyone else. I wasn't a drug dealer or an assassin. I hadn't taken anything that wasn't mine other than a name.

I wasn't on the run from the law because there was a warrant out for my arrest for some previous crime. I was on the run from the law because my husband *was* the law, and he wanted me dead.

Telling him any or all of that meant trusting him, and he'd proved I couldn't. He'd lied to me about things more important than a name. Had I not overheard that conversation, he would have helped the police find me and take my fingerprints by force.

But I also couldn't stand the thought that he'd be assuming the worst of me—that I'd taken part in some other horrible crime and that was why I didn't want the police to have my fingerprints.

"I possess identification with a name on it other than my own."

I kept the statement formal, like what might show up on a police report. Keeping it formal was safer. I should have hung up this phone call long ago. I didn't owe him an explanation.

Another beat of near-silence, as if he were trying to either digest what I'd said or decide whether I was lying. Maybe both.

"How many?"

How many what? Ohh. How many fake names. "Just one. The one I go by. Isabel." I still didn't give him my last name. He'd only use it against me. And yet I still stupidly felt the need to explain why I'd have even one. "It was the only way to protect myself from a bad person who wanted to hurt me."

He could interpret that however he wanted—that I was a

drug dealer's girlfriend who knew too much, that I was a witness who didn't want to testify because I was afraid. He might even figure out that I was on the run from an abuser or a stalker, assuming he believed me.

"Then come back," Dan said. "If you didn't do anything wrong, you don't need to keep running. I'll help you figure this all out."

Yeah, right. And Jarrod was truly sorry every time he hurt me and promised to never do it again. I'd believed that for too many years and look where it got me.

I wouldn't let myself be fooled again. The only one I could trust was myself. "Is that why you lied to me about being a police officer?"

I couldn't keep the anger out of my voice. But I had the uncomfortable feeling, like my skin was too tight, that it wasn't only him I was mad at. I was mad at me, too. I'd put myself into another position where someone could hurt me.

"I didn't lie to you," Dan said. "You never asked what I did for a living. I just didn't tell you the truth."

Those were the kind of semantics Jarrod liked to use, too. "So are you a police officer?"

"A detective, yes. I worked undercover until my brother died, then I moved back to Lakeshore and took a job in homicide."

That explained why he was so hard to read and was so good at adapting his personality to fit. Just when I thought I couldn't feel stupider, I did. He must have figured out that I was lonely and loved children, and he played me. Just like Jarrod. "Are you working your grandfather's case?"

"Not officially. It'd be a conflict of interest. But I couldn't sit back and do nothing, either. A buddy of mine's lead on the case, and he's keeping me filled in."

Was that a hint of pleading in his voice?

Even if it were, he could be faking that, too. "But you were trying to prove I'd done it." *Don't let your voice crack,* I prompted myself. *Keep it together.* "That's why you offered to work as a team."

"I wasn't sure."

It was as good as admitting that everything I'd thought was real—the real trust, the real caring for my health—hadn't been.

It didn't matter. I was on the road again. I had a plan. Soon nothing that happened in Lakeshore would matter.

The noise in the background had stopped. He must have pulled over as well and switched the call to his phone from his car. "We checked out Amy Miller. She's the wife of an FBI agent. She's been missing for over a year."

My throat went raw. He knew. "Did you talk to her husband?"

He made an affirmative noise. "He's worried about her. He thinks she may have gotten into something dangerous that she didn't know how to get out of. He wants to know she's safe and to have her come home no matter what she's done."

Forget repainting and new plates. I had to scuttle the truck as soon as I reached Detroit.

"Her husband's a liar."

I disconnected the call and pulled back out onto the road. I'd have enough money to pick up a new name and get myself a bus or a train ticket to somewhere else. Maybe even to Canada, where Jarrod would have no authority.

CHAPTER 21

Fake identities were harder to come by in Detroit than I'd thought they would be. A day later, I still didn't have a new identity. The only thing I'd managed to do since leaving Lakeshore was dump my old phone and get a new one, with a new number.

My trouble with buying a new identity might have been because I didn't have the connections here to find the right people. In Florida, I'd been staying in a woman's shelter. I wasn't the only one who wanted to disappear rather than hope I wouldn't become a statistic. One of the employees quietly facilitated that for women who wanted it.

Here, everyone I asked looked at me like I had to be working for the police. No one wanted to admit to anything, and I wasn't brave enough to go into the parts of Detroit where someone might. The one guy I had managed to find showed me product that looked like it'd only fool a cashier if you were underage and wanted to buy beer or cigarettes.

Every additional day I waited was one more day that the police might find me. Jarrod had even won over Dan with his sad story.

I had to leave my truck and get a new identity somewhere else. Staying with my truck any longer had become too great a risk.

I parked it on a street where half the houses were boarded up. If I were lucky, someone would see it and decide it'd be worth stealing. If and when it was found, that would provide an extra layer of confusion that could allow me the time to get a new identity.

I rifled through each drawer, taking out anything important that would fit in a duffle bag. It was shocking how much I *didn't* have. Most of my belongings were cooking gear for the truck or too big to carry along, like the portable heater I'd starved for weeks to be able to afford. I'd accumulated a few too many clothes to take along, but not even enough to fill up a small closet. I had a handwritten thank-you card from Nicole from her wedding and my dad's old Bible. Nothing else mattered.

I climbed out of the back of my truck and slammed the door shut. I'd leave the back locked, but the front unlocked and the keys in the glove box.

I went around to the front of my truck and popped the glove box open.

A paper fluttered out.

The part of me that had learned to be neat to survive living in such a tight space couldn't stand to leave it lying on the floor even if I was abandoning the truck. I picked it up.

It was the invitation to Janie's school play. The smiling cat on the front looked like he was laughing at me. Words at the bottom that I hadn't noticed before seemed to jump off the page.

Family and student party to follow. Please bring a dessert to share. No nuts or bananas allowed.

My duffle bag suddenly felt like I'd loaded it up with rocks, not clothes. I lowered it to the ground and gripped the invitation with both hands.

No nuts allowed.

The thing that I couldn't figure out, that had been bothering me since Janie and I were almost run down by the car, tried to wriggle to the surface.

Her class had a picnic earlier this year, Dan had said when he called me about baking something for Janie's play, *and she almost ate a brownie with nuts in it because someone forgot and didn't label them properly.*

What were the odds that Janie would almost die from her nut allergy twice in such a short span of time when both her school and her family knew that she couldn't eat them?

And then almost be run down by a car.

One near-death experience was a tragedy. Two near-death

experiences could be a weird coincidence. Three near-death experiences made a pattern.

I slumped against the side of my truck. Janie's questions about secrets might not have been only because she heard Dan telling someone he thought I was keeping secrets. She came to talk to me about secrets because I was someone who *also* had a secret. She'd been reaching out, too afraid to come right out and say anything after she'd been accused of lying.

She knew something—something someone made her promise to keep secret, but felt threatened enough by to kill her over. Janie had been the real target all along. Harold Cartwright had been the innocent collateral damage.

The police were looking in the wrong direction for the killer. Even if Dan convinced them it was someone trying to hurt him, they'd be looking in the wrong direction. They might not realize the true target until the killer succeeded in killing Janie. Even after that, they might continue to think it was about someone from Dan's past wanting to get even with him. As a former undercover cop, he no doubt had many dangerous enemies.

I had to call Dan.

I pulled my phone out of my pocket. Then called myself every name I could think of and some I made up.

I didn't have Dan's phone number in my new phone. It'd been stored in my old phone. The one I'd tossed into a dumpster yesterday after buying this one.

Maybe there was another way to get his phone number. I opened the internet browser on my new phone and went to the 411 online phonebook. I typed in Dan's name.

He wasn't listed.

Claire might be. I changed my search for her name. No results.

Arg. Of course there wouldn't be. Claire's legal name wasn't Claire Cartwright. I knew her as Claire Cartwright because I'd met her after her husband left her and she started using her maiden name again.

I pulled up Harold Cartwright's obituary. VanDyke. Claire VanDyke.

I put her name into the 411 search. Michael and Claire VanDyke came up. I called the number. The phone rang six times before sending me to a message in Claire's voice that sounded like it'd been recorded on a traditional landline answering machine. I left a message.

Her cell phone wasn't listed.

And since I never thought I'd need it again, I'd thrown out the paper Alan Brooksbank gave me with Blake's phone number on it.

I couldn't call the police. All I had was a hunch. The Lakeshore police wouldn't give out a detective's number to some random, anonymous woman calling for it. They'd make me leave a message.

That might be too late. If the car that almost ran her down was intentional, the killer was getting desperate.

The only solution I could think of involved going back to the dumpster where I'd thrown my phone and digging around to see if it was still there. While I knew dumpster-diving was a thing some people did, rotten meat made me squeamish. The smell and the maggots and...

I swallowed hard and turned my mind away. Maybe I shouldn't think about what I might find in the dumpster along with my phone. I put my truck into drive and headed back out onto the road.

The dumpster was in a part of Detroit near the airport, behind a pizza place. I'd chosen it because it seemed low-traffic, and I didn't want to be spotted dumping my phone. Hopefully that meant I also wouldn't be spotted trying to retrieve it.

I parked beside the dumpster, effectively blocking any garbage truck that came by to empty it. People died every year from dumpster diving. I wasn't about to become one of them.

I took my last breath of clean air and climbed up into the dumpster. Flies buzzed up off the black garbage bags, disturbed by my entrance. My eyes watered and bile burned up into my throat.

Breathe through your mouth, I reminded myself.

But I'd have sworn that when I did that, I could taste the smell instead. At least if I threw up in here, I wouldn't have to clean it up.

The dumpster was fuller than I remembered by a quarter. That meant my phone would be down a layer.

A dumpster wasn't the best place for methodical sorting. I moved the bags of garbage from one side to the other, and then felt around in the clearing I'd made. Some of the bags tipped back into the hole.

This wasn't going to work. I'd have to move the bags out and back in again. I hefted eight bags out. My shoulders and back spasmed, and the dumpster felt like it was swaying. It had to be from my lack of food. I hadn't eaten anything since leaving Lakeshore yesterday.

I lifted two more bags. My phone still wasn't in sight. Could it have tumbled down into the very bottom? The garbage was up above my knees. If I had to remove everything, I'd collapse first.

I stuck my hand down between the remaining bags and felt around. My fingers hit something squishy. I jerked back, and my hand came up covered in red goo.

"It's probably pizza sauce or ketchup." I spoke out loud to myself, hoping hearing the words would convince me.

I stared at my hand.

Ketchup. The red rectangle with the white label on Janie's drawing had been a ketchup bottle. The thing that represented her great-grandpa's birthday barbeque to Janie was the special ketchup that they always had.

That meant that whoever wrote the description for her probably knew exactly what kind of ketchup Claire would have at the birthday party—and they wouldn't have known that she couldn't get it.

Someone from Janie's school would have also known about her allergy, and the first "accidental" nut inclusion had happened at a school event.

Even the accusation that Janie had lied fit. Whoever had asked her to keep a secret might also want to discredit her to make sure that, even if she told someone before they could kill her, no one would believe her because she had a history of lying.

My stomach rolled, but this time it wasn't because of the smell around me. If I were right, the killer would likely try again at the play after-party today. It was the perfect opportunity. All they had to do was make a snack they knew Janie would want and label it nut-free. With all the different families and guests, there'd be no way to tell exactly who'd done it.

I checked my watch. Three-thirty. The play was less than two hours away.

CHAPTER 22

I tossed more bags from the dumpster, ignoring the screaming in my muscles and my body's cringe reflex as something living moved in the corner. It was probably only a mouse. A mouse couldn't hurt me.

I still couldn't find my phone. A dumpster diver might have already found it and taken it. Or this could be a single day's garbage and the load with my phone was gone. The stench suggested the former was the more likely explanation. Whatever the cause, I didn't see my phone. Maybe it was so covered in fluid that my eyes were skimming over it in the shadows cast by the building and the sides of the dumpster.

There had to be a solution here, another way to get Dan's phone number even if I couldn't find my phone.

I crawled back out of the dumpster and washed my hands in the sink in the back of my truck. I forced myself to take a few deep breaths and center myself the way I used to when I knew Jarrod was trying to wind me up. Whose number did I know?

The only one I'd saved before tossing my old phone was Nicole's. As a criminal defense attorney, she might have resources to find an unlisted phone number that I didn't.

I'd promised myself that I wouldn't put her in danger by giving her even a hint of where I was. This once, I'd have to break that promise. Nicole would want me to knowing a child's life could be in danger.

One ring. Two.

Please pick up. Please pick up.

It'd been such a long time since I'd prayed, but it was the only thing I could think to do. If this didn't work...

"Nicole Fitzhenry-Dawes." Still Fitzhenry-Dawes professionally, even though she'd changed her name after she got married.

I let out a gush of air from the breath I hadn't realized I was holding. "I need help." I explained the situation to her without enough of a pause for her to even ask what was wrong. "Can you find an unlisted cell phone number? The person I'm looking for is Dan Holmes of the Lakeshore police."

"When you helped me when you were here and said you couldn't let other people be hurt without anyone to turn to, I didn't think you'd take it this far. This is the second crime you've ended up tangled up in since Fair Haven."

I hadn't thought I'd end up this way, either. The harder I

tried to stay away from the police, the more I seemed to end up right in their path.

"I'll put in some calls," Nicole said. "But I don't know how long it might take."

I thanked her and disconnected, then braced myself and climbed back into the dumpster. Until Nicole called with a number, I'd keep looking.

I HAD ALL THE BAGS OUT OF THE DUMPSTER AND WAS RIFLING through the loose trash at the bottom when my new phone rang. I wiped my grimy hand on my equally grimy jeans, then gave up and answered my phone anyway.

"I have the number for you," Nicole said without bothering with a hello. "I had to call Erik, but he was able to contact the Lakeshore PD and convince them to give it to him. I'm sorry it took as long as it did. Erik said they made him jump through hoops to prove he was who he said he was first."

I didn't care that it'd taken a few minutes extra so long as I had the number.

I had Nicole wait while I exited the dumpster again and got something to write the number down. I thanked her and disconnected.

Once I got a hold of Dan, I'd rest for a minute and then return all the trash to the dumpster. It wasn't fair of me to leave it there for the garbage men to have to pick up when they'd come expecting to simply dump the dumpster into their truck and move on.

The play was only an hour and a half from starting now.

I dialed the number Nicole gave me. The phone went instantly to voicemail.

No. No, no, no. He must have already turned his phone off for the play. Either that or he didn't answer unknown numbers.

I called back. "It's Isabel. Janie's in danger. I need you to call me right away."

I left my new phone number.

You've done your due diligence, Fear said. *Now you need to take care of yourself and run.*

Maybe Fear was right and wise, but going further away before I knew Janie was safe left my stomach feeling like I had food poisoning, worse even than I'd felt from getting a big whiff of the rotting garbage.

Dan might not turn his phone back on immediately after the play finished. If I was right that someone at her school was behind this, he might receive my message too late.

But the only other way to reach him was to go back. Going back ensured that the police would catch me. Allowing the police to catch me and identify me as Amy Miller, potentially keeping me in a holding cell until they could decide whether to charge me with Harold's murder or not, meant Jarrod was sure to come for me.

He'd pay my bail, take me away, and then no one would ever see me again. Everyone would believe I'd jumped bail, leaving my devoted husband in the lurch. No one would think he'd killed me.

But my other alternative was to risk letting a little girl die to save myself.

I hadn't been brave enough to leave Jarrod when I was pregnant. My fear and my hope that he'd change for the baby kept me there. It cost my child's life.

I'd seen my rescue of Janie before as a small atonement. If I ran now instead of going back, it'd be worse than what I'd done to my baby because I knew what would happen if Dan didn't get my message in time.

Jarrod might find me and kill me, but at least I'd die knowing I'd done the right thing.

I had to go back to Lakeshore.

CHAPTER 23

I drove faster than the speed limit back to Lakeshore. It'd taken me almost two hours to get from Lakeshore to Detroit yesterday. I had half that time to get back now.

Avoiding a ticket was the least of my worries. My suspicion could be entirely wrong. This might all be pointless in the end. But it didn't feel wrong. It all made sense.

I didn't know which teacher or volunteer Janie might know the secret about, but the most important thing was to make sure she was safe. After that, Dan could explain it all to Detective Labreck, and they could get a warrant for the fingerprints of everyone who worked with Janie's class. Even if Claire had invited one of them to the party—which was unlikely—they'd have a hard time explaining why their fingerprints were on all the bottles. Coupled with whatever damaging secret Janie knew, it should be enough for an arrest.

Even if it wasn't enough to immediately lead to an arrest, Janie would be safe once the secret was out and the police had a suspect. Whoever it was might try to flee, but they weren't likely to still kill Janie at that point.

I called Dan three more times on the drive. His phone went directly to voicemail each time.

My gas tank needle touched red, but I was sure I didn't have time to fuel up. How long would a children's play last? Half an hour at most?

All the parking spots near the theater where the invitation said the play was taking place were full by the time I got there. My truck made a sputtering noise right before I turned it off, like it'd finally drunk up the last drop of gasoline.

Wooden blocks propped the front doors open, and a Bristol board sign declared the play's name and time. The cat on this one was in color—black and white with a red sock on his head.

I jogged down the hallway, following the paw-print signs to the auditorium. The doors were closed. Two men wearing bowties stood outside the doors. Based on the fact that they both held a stack of folded papers that looked like programs, they had to be either working for the theater or for the school as ushers.

As I got close, they both turned in my direction. The skinnier one backed away two steps and pressed a hand over his mouth and nose.

The other's gaze jumped from my face to my feet and back

again. Unlike his partner, he stepped sideways, blocking my access to the auditorium. "May we help you?"

I glanced down at my clothes. Food leftovers that even I couldn't identify covered the front of my shirt and smeared my jeans in an array of red, brown, darker brown, and greenish brown. Based on the reaction of the man who'd backed away, I probably stank like rotting meat and moldy potatoes. Somewhere on the drive, I'd gone nose-blind to the stench.

My gut reaction was to slink away. My appearance and smell would draw everyone's attention to me. But I didn't have time to find a sneaky way around them or to clean up.

"I'm looking for..." What was the name of Janie's teacher again? It'd been on the door under her picture. "I'm looking for Ms. Glover's class."

The skinny man made a gagging noise and edged even further away.

The other man—whose eyebrows reminded me of corn silk—broadened his stance. "Are you a parent?"

I was a mom, even if my baby hadn't lived. He hadn't asked if I was a parent of one of the children here. "Yes."

He opened up the program. "Which child?"

Either I'd hesitated too long in my answer or my smell made me seem like a liar. Now I would have to lie, but at this point scruples seemed to favor stopping a murder over telling the truth. "Janie Holmes." I swiped my hands down the front of my shirt. "I didn't have time to shower after I got off work, but I can't miss her play."

"Where do you work?" the gagging man whispered, almost under his breath. "A sewage treatment plant?"

I'd had to act while with Jarrod, pretending things didn't hurt when they did and that I agreed with him when I didn't. Maybe those skills could extend a little further to pretending confidence and bravado when I didn't feel it.

I flashed the skinny usher a grin. "How'd you know? We had a line break today or I would have been here earlier."

The ushers exchanged a look that said *Is she a nutter or telling the truth?* It was almost as if they didn't know whether it was easier to believe that I was a sewage plant worker who came to her daughter's play covered in human filth or that I was a delusional homeless person who was quick-witted enough to come up with that story.

It gave me an idea. I moved as if to open the door. "I was thinking I'd just say hi to Janie and then try to grab a shower at home before the family party, but I could go take a seat if you think that'd be better."

You'd have thought I dangled a dead mouse in front of skinny usher's nose based on his face. He scooted over next to the usher who was playing the role of human wall, put his hand up to the man's ear, and started whispering.

Without super hearing, I couldn't tell what he was saying. Best guess it was something about how it'd ruined the entire play if they let me in there. People would have to move because they wouldn't be able to sit next to me, and how were they ever supposed to get the smell out of the cushioned seats?

Skinny guy backed away again.

Blockade usher didn't relinquish his place. "Down the hall to the left. Each grade has their own room, so you'll need to find your daughter's class on your own."

As I turned away, I caught a glimpse of them huddle-talking again. They could be deciding whether to call the police just in case.

I had to move fast.

Only one grown-up spotted me as I hustled from room to room. From the double-take she did, she'd be calling someone if the ushers didn't. One room was empty except for children's belongings. That class was probably playing its part on the stage. Based on the music filtering softly down the hallway, the play was a musical. Some of the older students likely had speaking roles, and the younger classes must each have a musical number.

The next room, I peeked around the edge of the doorway and spotted the teacher's assistant from Janie's class. The kids were lined up, singing, presumably practicing their part one last time before they went on stage.

Janie wasn't with them.

CHAPTER 24

I pulled my head back out of sight.

Maybe Janie had a special role and that's why she wasn't in the room. But wouldn't Dan have mentioned that when he invited me to the play?

It was also possible that Janie had taken sick today, and they weren't here at all. But then why wouldn't Dan have answered his phone?

I walked casually by the room, looking in as I passed.

Janie wasn't the only one missing. The teacher's assistant was there, but her teacher wasn't. This wasn't the kind of event a teacher handed off to someone else.

If my suspicions were correct, her teacher could be the one who wanted her dead. She might have already taken Janie somewhere.

The question was where. My heart felt like it was beating faster than the second hand on a watch.

I continued down the hall, looking into each room as I passed. Janie wasn't in any of them.

I had to stop and think rather than continuing to run blindly around. This building was too big for me to check every nook and cranny.

Whoever was behind this had taken great pains to cover their tracks. They wanted this to look like an accident. There were limited ways to make a child's death look like an accident in a building like this. They could push her down a flight of stairs. Or they could stick to their original plan and feed her something with nuts in it.

Given how many people would be bringing food, it'd be easy for someone to claim that Janie had gotten something that someone had accidentally put a nut product into. If the killer were smart, they wouldn't leave fingerprints behind on their baked good this time.

I'd seen a sign at the last hallway I passed, pointing to the reception hall. That seemed like the best bet for where the desserts would be waiting.

The hallway was empty. I sprinted down it.

The doors to the reception hall were closed. I tugged on one, and it opened. I burst through the doors, not sure exactly what I expected to find.

I hadn't expected an empty room. The food was there in

Tupperware containers and plates covered in Saran Wrap. I walked alongside it—chocolate chip cookies, lemon bars, cherry tarts, at least three batches of brownies. Nothing screamed *I hold deadly nuts*, but I hadn't expected it to stand out.

A faint scuffling noise came from somewhere behind me.

I spun around. The room still seemed to be empty, but there was another door at the end next to the fire exit. The sign on the door read *Janitor*.

A small squeak that sounded like an injured mouse came from behind the door. It might be machinery, but I'd come this far and drawn this much attention to myself already. Barging into a janitorial closet only to find a janitor or an actual mouse wouldn't make it much worse.

I threw the door open.

The "closet" turned out to be more of a room. Three slop sinks lined the back along with a large industrial vacuum cleaner and another machine I didn't recognize.

A woman faced the corner of the room between the strange piece of machinery and the wall. I couldn't see her face or what was behind her, but I had a good guess.

"What are you doing?" I tried to shout, but my voice came out weak, the same way it had the few times I'd tried to stand up to Jarrod.

It must have been enough. The woman pivoted around. She was an athletic forty-something, and she held a brownie in one hand.

The image was so ludicrous I almost couldn't believe what I was seeing.

Janie hunched behind her, both hands over her mouth. She looked up and dropped her hands. "Isabel!"

The way she said my name made my heart feel like it'd been crushed under a rolling pin. It carried a lot of fear. And hope. Like maybe she was safe because I was there.

The woman didn't move. There was almost an unnatural calm about her. Despite the dim lighting and her hair being longer than it was in the picture on Janie's classroom door, I recognized her as Janie's teacher. Ms. Glover, according to the name tag beneath the sign.

We stared each other down. The look she gave me reminded me of someone staring down a snake when they weren't sure whether it was poisonous or not.

"You'll need to leave. I'm in the middle of disciplining a student."

The note of authority in her voice was strong enough that my spine felt turned to soup.

I glanced at Janie. She had her knees up to her chest now. Her cheeks were wet. In the dim lighting, I couldn't tell if her cheeks were a normal color or flushed with the beginnings of a rash.

I wasn't leaving her here, no matter who ordered me. I inclined my head to one side. "With a brownie?"

"I caught her in here stealing things from the dessert tables. I took this from her. Something I'll discuss with her father later."

The implication was that I had no right to question her. Had I been anyone else, I probably would have believed her and left. Because kids sneaked food, especially dessert. I'd done it as a child.

And maybe she was telling the truth, but the look on Janie's face said otherwise.

I moved a step farther into the room and made sure Janie saw that I wasn't leaving. "Is that true?"

She shot a glance at Ms. Glover and shook her head.

Ms. Glover didn't even look back to see how she'd answered. "We've had to talk to Janie before about lying. I see these types of behaviors a lot in children from single-parent homes."

Heat filled my chest, heavy, like it wanted to boil over. "That's not always true. I was raised by a single dad."

Ms. Glover pursed her lips and ran her gaze over me. "I'm not surprised."

If she hoped to throw me off by insulting me, it wasn't going to work. Janie didn't want to be here. I was sure my fears were right about what was going on, but even if they weren't, this wasn't how it should be done.

"If you think she's acting out because she's from a single-parent home, then it'd be better to talk to her dad about what's going on." I held out my hand toward Janie. "Come here, and we'll go find your dad."

Janie launched to her feet.

Ms. Glover spun around and pointed at the floor. "Sit."

Janie hesitated, not sitting, but not coming closer to me, either.

She was clearly afraid, but she'd also been taught to respect adults and obey her teacher.

The low hum from the back of the room cut out. In the silence, I could hear Janie's breathing.

She was wheezing. It wasn't as pronounced as when I'd found her at Harold's party, but it was still there.

Ms. Glover had already forced her to take a bite before I'd gotten there.

Which meant she was stalling. She knew that if she could wait long enough, Janie would die. There'd be nothing I could do to help her. Her little backpack where she kept her epi pen was nowhere in sight.

The machine creating the hum kicked back on, drowning out Janie's labored breathing again.

I had to call her bluff. "She's having an allergic reaction to something. She needs help."

Something flickered across Ms. Glover's face that looked like recognition. "You're the woman from the article. You were at the outdoor birthday party. Where you failed the first time to kill Janie, and then had to pretend to save her when someone spotted you. You came back to finish the job tonight. I found you, but I wasn't in time this time. No one will believe you over me."

Janie whimpered.

She's right, Fear said. *No one's going to believe you.*

I'd always thought sometimes Fear's voice sounded a lot like a voice I should know. I recognized it this time. It was Jarrod's voice.

I'd listened to that line for too many years. This time, I wasn't going to listen.

Dan would believe me over this woman. He'd have my back, not someone else's. I had to trust that he would, or both Janie and I were done for.

I eased a step toward them. "Janie's dad will believe me. He's a homicide detective, so the other police will believe him."

If Janie died, it wouldn't even matter if anyone believed me or not. I'd have failed.

I couldn't let that be how this ended, regardless of what happened to me. Ms. Glover might kill me and tell her story to everyone and they might believe her, but if even Dan believed me, Janie would be safe.

I dove for Ms. Glover. "Run for your dad!" I shouted to Janie.

I didn't even have time to pray that she made it to a grown-up who could help her before I was grappling with Ms. Glover on the ground.

Her knee connected with my rib. My body instinctively

curled into a protective ball rather than fighting back. I didn't know how to fight. I only knew how to hide.

What had saved me before would get me killed now if she found something heavy to crack me in the head with.

She kicked me again, hard enough to knock the air from my lungs. Then backed off.

She was reaching for something. I had to move.

I rolled to the side. A wrench connected with the concrete floor where I'd been.

"It'll be self-defense," Ms. Glover said. "You were trying to hurt a student of mine, and I caught you at it."

I dragged myself to my feet. My ribs screamed like they'd been pried apart. I turned my mind away from it, imagining my protective brick wall, and limped backward. Somehow in our roll across the floor, she'd managed to get between me and the door.

Rushing her now that she had a weapon seemed stupid. Waiting for her to hit me with the wrench also didn't seem smart. All I had to block with were my bare arms. A good blow from a wrench would break my bone. It wouldn't be my first broken bone—I knew how long a bone took to heal and the challenge it added to everything. I couldn't be on the run, living on the street, with a broken bone.

My back hit the wall. I might not have defensive skills, but I'd talked my way out of a potential beating more than once. This time, I only needed to stall long enough for help to arrive.

Help was coming. I had to believe help would come. Dan would come.

"It'll be too late for you no matter what story you tell them," I said.

Her grip on the wrench twitched, but she kept moving toward me. She might think I was trying to distract her so I could charge her or grab for something to defend myself. I would have grabbed my own weapon if I could, but the only things near me were sponges and rags. They'd bounce right off of her.

"They'll take your fingerprints even with that story you've made up. They'll match the ones on the ketchup you tampered with." I slowly drew my truck keys out of my pocket and dangled them in front of her. "You'd be better off getting a head start now."

The wrench lowered a couple of inches. "I'm not stupid enough to think you'd help me escape."

I shrugged. "I don't want to die. I just didn't want to allow a little girl to die either."

Even though I had no intention of actually allowing her to get away, she must have heard the truth in my reasoning.

She let go of the wrench with one hand and held her hand up. "Toss them here."

Blood pounded behind my eyes. She was smart. It was possible she planned to try to attack me while my guard was momentarily down. Not for the first time, I wished I could read body language better. I couldn't tell if she was playing me while I was trying to play her.

My best way to find out was to throw the keys slightly toward the hand with the wrench. If she moved to grab them, I could sprint to her other side. If she didn't, then I'd have to dive and try to get behind the industrial vacuum cleaner.

I tossed the keys, and she leapt toward me, swinging the wrench. I dove to the side, smashing into the vacuum and toppling over, tangled in the cord.

I was done. All I could hope now was that she'd hit me directly in the temple, killing me instantly.

"Drop it," Dan's voice was so loud that, for a second, I thought he was standing beside me.

Ms. Glover dropped the wrench. It hit the ground with a clang and a strange bounce.

Dan stepped through the doorway, a gun in his hand focused on Ms. Glover. "Are you okay?" he asked.

It took me a full ten seconds before my mind sorted through everything enough to figure out he was talking to me even though he never took his gaze off Ms. Glover.

"I'm fine. Janie?"

"Claire had an epi pen in her purse. An ambulance and backup are on their way."

A quiver started in my legs and rode up my body. I'd known what coming back would mean. But preparing for something and having that thing happen often weren't the same thing. I felt a bit like I only had a few weeks left to live, and there were so many things left I still wanted to do.

Dan nodded toward the doorway. "Go. I'll find you afterward."

I looked toward the door and back to him. His back was to me now. He motioned for Ms. Glover to turn around, and he pulled out a pair of handcuffs.

He was letting me go? How would that work? Surely the police would need my statement.

Dan glanced back over his shoulder and raised both eyebrows. I didn't need to be told twice. I strode as fast as my aching body would take me out of the building through the back door and to my truck.

Dan had said he'd find me. That seemed like the place he was most likely to look. And I couldn't have left before that even if I'd wanted to. My keys lay somewhere on the janitor's closet floor, and my truck had no gas.

I sat on the curb next to my truck, watching from a distance as emergency vehicles pulled up and parents with their children filed out. Definitely not the way they would have expected their special end-of-the-year play to go. Had the stakes been less than life and death, I would have felt guilty for ruining their evening.

Almost an hour passed before Dan came out of the building. He looked around, and he must have spotted my hard-to-miss truck despite how far down the street I was. He headed in my direction.

Ten feet from me, Dan pulled my keys from his pocket. "I promised Labreck I'd take your statement, so if I give these back, you have to promise not to skip town."

"I won't leave before you get what you need." If I had my freedom to leave after that, though, I still had to leave.

Dan's expression didn't give away whether he caught my slight dodge or not. He moved a step closer to where I sat, my keys still in his hand. "Were you really going to let her get away?"

I flinched inside. I must have sounded like a coward. "You heard that?"

"As I was sneaking up to the door to assess the situation."

Maybe it would be better if he believed I would let a murderer go free to save myself. Maybe then he wouldn't try to convince me to stay. Maybe he'd even help me leave.

Jarrod had always made sure I knew how weak and selfish I was. It shouldn't bother me if Dan felt the same way. I'd never see him again once I left town.

But I couldn't make the lie come out. Putting that black mark on what I'd done made me feel like I would have if I'd baked a beautiful wedding cake and then hit it with a sledgehammer.

Instead I got up, took the keys back, and put them in my pocket. "You're going to need to drive me to a gas station. I'm pretty sure my tank doesn't have enough in it to start, let alone make it down the street."

Dan smirked. Instead of making me sick to my stomach the way a similar expression on Jarrod's face would have, I actually found it a bit endearing. There was a softness to Dan's smirk, like we were sharing an inside joke.

He spread his arms out as if to block me from heading for his car. "I'll go fill a can and bring it back to you. I don't know what you have all over you, but I'd rather it not end up all over my seats."

CHAPTER 25

I emerged from Dan's guest bathroom, showered and
freshly dressed, at the same time as Dan came out of his
bedroom, where Janie had insisted on sleeping for the
night. I couldn't blame her for not wanting to sleep in her own
room alone after everything that happened. Dan might have a
difficult time convincing her to go back to school even though
her teacher wouldn't be there anymore.

He closed the door softly behind him. "She and Claire are
both asleep. Looks like I'm sleeping on the couch or in Janie's
princess bed."

He didn't move any further toward me, but something in his
posture made me think he wanted to hug me. I slipped past him
and down the stairs.

He trailed along behind me. "Hot chocolate?"

I could use a cup of something sweet. I only drank coffee and tea for the caffeine, not because I particularly enjoyed them. "This time I'll make it for you."

I had to run out to my truck for cocoa, vanilla, and cinnamon. Dan apparently had been telling the truth when he called saying he needed help with a dessert. He could cook, but he couldn't bake, so he didn't have some of the things I considered staples in the house. He did have sugar, at least, since he used it in his coffee.

He hopped up on the island in the kitchen and watched me work. "Is this going to spoil me for the packaged stuff?"

I smiled at him over my shoulder. "I hope so. It's my grandma's recipe. She refused to drink any other hot chocolate the same way your grandpa refused to use any other ketchup."

Dan chuckled. It was a comforting thing to hear someone else's genuine laughter. My truck got silent as a morgue when I closed up for the day and was there alone.

I'd probably miss the silence, too, once I left my truck behind. Finding Harold's killer hadn't changed the fact that I still needed to disappear. Jarrod knew where I was. "What happens next? Will they arrest her?"

"Labreck texted me while I was putting Janie to bed. The computer confirmed a match between Ms. Glover's prints and the ones on the ketchup bottles. They've charged her with murder and attempted murder. Now they'll start taking statements."

That could end up being a massive undertaking in preparation for court. They could easily interview the child Janie caught Ms. Glover taking inappropriate pictures of, but they'd also have to talk to every student who was in one of her classes. They'd also need Claire to confirm that Ms. Glover hadn't been invited to Harold's party.

The bubbles in my pot rose up the sides, reminding me to pay attention. I turned the heat down. Scorched hot cocoa tasted worse than the cheapest packaged hot chocolate brand.

"They'll want to start with Janie and you," Dan said.

He still didn't understand. He thought whatever was going on between Jarrod and I could be easily fixed. He thought that whatever trouble I'd gotten myself into, I could get out of with his and Jarrod's help. He might even think that testifying against Ms. Glover was the way to get leniency for whatever hypothetical crimes I'd committed.

He had no idea I'd be long gone by morning.

Except… "Do you think they'll need my testimony to convict her?"

Dan slid down off the counter, his long legs making the drop barely noticeable. "Depends on how much other evidence they can find. If more than one child speaks up and if they can find a grocery store receipt showing she bought the ketchup, you won't be as important."

I turned off the heat under the pot and filled two mugs. Dan motioned for me to bring them to the breakfast nook. I followed him and set them on the table, but I didn't sit.

Not as important wasn't the same as *not important* or *not needed.*

"I can't stay and testify. I can't even give the police a statement."

He gave me a smile that I imagined had disarmed the defenses of many criminals while he was undercover. "We can ask the district attorney to give you immunity for the fake ID. Your husband—"

"My husband is the reason I can't stay. Not now that he knows where I am." Unfortunately for Dan, I was warier than most criminals, and that was saying something.

"Okay." Dan nudged my mug of hot cocoa toward the other side of the table. "Will you at least sit? You're making me feel like you're going to run if I blink wrong."

My whole body ached from being tensed to do just that. I lowered into the chair across from him and slid the mug of cocoa toward me. "Maybe not if you blink wrong."

Dan's smile this time was less charming but more genuine, like this one came from his heart rather than from his head.

Seeing it brought my shields down a little more.

"Do you want to tell me why you're working so hard to hide?" he asked.

I did and I didn't. I did because I wanted him to know that I wasn't overreacting. And I didn't because he might think I was overreacting. He was a cop. The thin blue line wasn't only a cliché. It was something they lived by.

I wasn't completely sure that the few days he'd known me would be enough to guarantee he'd take my side instead of another officer of the law's. Having him stick up for me today had sent a warmth into my middle that went deeper than the hot cocoa could reach, and it felt too good to risk shattering that feeling so soon.

I shook my head. "Not yet." I added the *yet* as an olive branch.

Dan finally took a drink from his mug. His eyes drifted shut. "You're right. I am going to be spoiled. It's a good thing Janie didn't try this or I'd never hear the end of why couldn't I make hot cocoa like Isabel." He set the mug back down, but didn't let go of the handle, as if he didn't want to risk me taking it away. "Are you willing to work together on this to find a solution?"

I didn't know how to do this talking-to-a-man-as-an-equal thing. With my dad, I'd been his daughter even when I was his caretaker. With Jarrod, I couldn't have a discussion. He gave orders, and I was expected to follow them.

"I'm willing to try."

He paused for another drink of hot cocoa. "Glover probably won't take a plea deal. She has to know it won't go well for her in prison for a child crime. If this goes to court, we'll need your testimony to corroborate what Janie says about Ms. Glover trying to kill her tonight."

Otherwise it would be a teacher's word against a student. Ms. Glover's defense attorney could argue that Janie got caught sneaking snacks before the play and didn't want to be punished for it. They could also bring in that Janie had already been reprimanded at school for lying. Even though it was Ms. Glover who said Janie lied, the teacher's assistant had believed her at the time.

That alone wouldn't be enough to create reasonable doubt, but it opened a door. Ms. Glover's defense attorney would only need to find a few more inches to fling that door wide, and she'd walk out of it a free woman.

The problem was, if I stayed, I'd be dead before trial anyway. "My plan was to start over. New name. New career. New town."

Dan looked down into the depths of his mug. "Because of your husband."

"Because of my husband."

He looked back up, and his expression was hard to read again. Even understanding why he'd developed that ability, it was a frustrating quality. Even Nicole would have had a hard time reading him, and she seemed to be a human barometer.

"Will it be that easy for you to stop baking?"

It'd be like losing the last piece of my identity. "I wish you hadn't called Jarrod."

Dan's Adam's apple pulsed in his throat. "I didn't tell him the name you were using here or about your business."

I leaned back in my chair, clutching the mug to my chest to borrow some of its warmth. "He'll still come looking for me here. Eventually he'll find Alan Brooksbank's article online, he'll recognize me, and he'll know."

Dan took his mug to the sink and rinsed it out. His posture said *problem solved*, but that might have been something that had been trained into him as well.

He turned back around and leaned on the counter with his hands behind him. "I can have that article pulled. I can also call Amy's husband, and tell him that we don't know where his wife is but that we think she left town to avoid having to testify in a case where she was a witness."

Something bubbled in my chest, like my rib cage wanted to expand. His wording couldn't have been accidental. "Amy's husband?"

"Yeah. 'Cause I know an Isabel…"

"Addington. Isabel Addington."

He gave me that smile that made me think he felt it rather than that it was calculated to get the result he wanted. It was a smile that said he knew how big an act of trust that was. "I know an Isabel Addington, but I don't know where to find Amy Miller. I assume she skipped town."

Dan might be the one person who could fool Jarrod into believing I'd actually left Lakeshore. Dan had tricked whatever criminal syndicate he'd been asked to infiltrate in his undercover work. And Jarrod wouldn't expect a member of law enforcement to lie to him. He wouldn't expect I'd have confided in anyone in law enforcement after how many years he'd spent brainwashing me into believing that all of them would side with him.

There was only one flaw in the plan. "The DA will still want my real name, and I'll have to use my real name in court."

"When I talk to Jarrod, I'll tell him Amy was a witness, so he won't find anything new if he's able to access the case files."

"And what about when I have to testify? He'll be there, waiting."

"That's months away. It gives us time to figure out how to deal with it if you still want to stay hidden."

Dan's plan might be bold enough to work. Jarrod would continue his search for me everywhere but here. It wouldn't protect me forever, but it might in the short term. I'd be able to keep my truck. I'd be able to continue building up my clientele and get on better financial footing should I have to run again down the road.

Dan caught my gaze and held it. "You're safer here where you have friends than you'll be anywhere else."

Nicole had tried to tell me the same thing when she wanted me to stay in Fair Haven. She'd been worried about my health as well as my safety. I'd been worried about her safety in return. But maybe Dan's plan solved that for me in Lakeshore. Jarrod wouldn't rough up another police officer for information the way he might feel he could a civilian. Dan's story would have Jarrod believing he didn't know anything about my whereabouts anyway.

"Friends plural?"

"Well, there's me and Janie." He ticked them off on his

fingers. He must have realized how pathetic having only two friends sounded because he ticked another finger. "And Claire."

I raised an eyebrow at him. "Claire?"

His expression turned sheepish, like he was a little boy I'd caught stealing a cookie. "Eventually. She'll come around."

Maybe if we had decades rather than months. Still, for now at least, he'd won the argument over whether I'd stay or go. "I guess I'll have to stay then. I've always wanted to see pigs fly."

Harold Cartwright wasn't able to try his birthday "cake," but you can. If you're not allergic to nuts, feel free to add them! A 1/2 cup of chopped walnuts works great in this recipe.

To receive Isabel's Top 10 Tips for Amazing Cupcakes and two additional bonus recipes that go along with this story, sign up for my newsletter at www.subscribepage.com/cupcakes.

INGREDIENTS

Cake:

1 1/4 cups all-purpose flour

1 teaspoon cinnamon

3/4 teaspoon baking powder

3/4 teaspoon baking soda

1/4 teaspoon salt

3/4 cup packed brown sugar

2 large eggs, at room temperature

1/3 cup buttermilk, at room temperature

1/4 cup unsweetened applesauce

3 tablespoons vegetable oil

1 teaspoon vanilla

1 1/2 cups grated carrots

Icing:

8 oz cream cheese, softened

1/4 cup unsalted butter, softened

3 cups powdered sugar

1 teaspoon vanilla extract

1/8 teaspoon salt

INSTRUCTIONS:

To Make the Cake:

1. Preheat oven to 350 degrees F, and line a muffin tin with cupcake liners.

2. In a medium bowl, whisk together flour, cinnamon, baking powder, baking soda, and salt. Set aside.

3. In a large bowl, whisk together brown sugar, eggs, buttermilk, applesauce, oil, and vanilla.

4. Stir in grated carrots.

5. Add dry mixture to wet mixture. Mix until just combined.

6. Scoop batter into cupcake liners. Fill the liners 2/3 to 3/4 of the way full.

7. Bake for 18 minutes or until a toothpick inserted into the center comes out clean.

8. Remove to a wire rack to cool completely before frosting.

To Make the Icing:

9. In a large bowl, using a mixer on high, beat together cream cheese and butter until creamy.

10. Add powdered sugar, vanilla, and salt. Beat on low for 30 seconds (to keep the sugar from poofing out in your face), then increase the speed to high for 2 minutes.

11. Ice cooled cupcakes with frosting.

Makes 12 cupcakes.

LETTER FROM THE AUTHOR

I hope you enjoyed getting to know Isabel better and solving this mystery alongside her. I have many more stories planned for her. You'll be seeing a lot more of Dan, Claire, and Janie in the future too!

You might have caught that Nicole mentioned two murder investigations that Isabel was a part of after leaving Fair Haven.

When was this other murder? you might be wondering. *It must have happened sometime between when she left Fair Haven and now.*

It did. It's part of a two-book set called *Slay Bells Ringing*. The box set will also include a mystery that Nicole and her new husband solve on their honeymoon. (You didn't think she'd stay out of trouble just because it was her honeymoon, did you?)

If you want to know when the next Cupcake Truck mystery

releases, make sure to sign up for my newsletter at www.sub-scribepage.com/cupcakes.

And if you enjoyed this book, I'd really appreciate it if you'd leave an honest review on Amazon or Goodreads. Reviews help fellow readers know if this is a book they might enjoy. Even a short sentence helps!

Love,

Emily

MAPLE SYRUP MYSTERIES

Looking for something to read until the next Cupcake Truck Mystery comes out? Try Emily James' Maple Syrup Mysteries. This thirteen book series is complete and available in both print and ebook formats. The first four books are also available as audiobooks.

Criminal defense attorney Nicole Fitzhenry-Dawes thought that moving to the small Michigan tourist town of Fair Haven and taking over her uncle's maple syrup farm would keep her far away from murderers, liars, and criminals. She couldn't have been more wrong...

If you love small-town settings, quirky characters, and a dollop of romance, then you'll enjoy this amateur sleuth mystery series.

Pick up the whole series at https://smarturl.it/maplesyrupmysteries.

ABOUT THE AUTHOR

Emily James grew up watching TV shows like *Matlock*, *Monk*, and *Murder She Wrote*. (It's pure coincidence that they all begin with an M.) It was no surprise to anyone when she turned into a mystery writer.

Alongside being a writer, she's also a wife, an animal lover, and a new artist. She likes coffee and painting and drinking coffee while painting. She also enjoys cooking. She tries not to do that while painting because, well, you shouldn't eat paint.

Emily and her husband share their home with a blue Great Dane, six cats (all rescues), and a budgie (who is both the littlest and the loudest).

If you'd like to know as soon as Emily's next mystery releases, please join her newsletter list at www.subscribepage.com/cupcakes.

She also loves hearing from readers.

www.authoremilyjames.com
authoremilyjames@gmail.com